AF450282

BLOOD PRESSURE LOGBOOK

NAME : ____

DOCTOR : _____________________   PHONE : _____________________

BLOOD TYPE : _____________________   DOB : _____________________

BLOOD
PRESSURE LOGBOOK

WEEK .... **WEIGHT** ....

DATE	TIME	AM	PM	SYSTOLIC – UPPER NO –	SYSTOLIC – LOWER NO –	HEART RATE	NOTE
MONDAY		AM	PM				
TUESDAY		AM	PM				
WEDNESDAY		AM	PM				
THURSDAY		AM	PM				
FRIDAY		AM	PM				
SATURDAY		AM	PM				
SUNDAY		AM	PM				

WEEK .... **WEIGHT** ....

DATE	TIME	AM	PM	SYSTOLIC – UPPER NO –	SYSTOLIC – LOWER NO –	HEART RATE	NOTE
MONDAY		AM	PM				
TUESDAY		AM	PM				
WEDNESDAY		AM	PM				
THURSDAY		AM	PM				
FRIDAY		AM	PM				
SATURDAY		AM	PM				
SUNDAY		AM	PM				

BLOOD
PRESSURE LOGBOOK

WEEK .... WEIGHT ....

DATE	TIME	AM	PM	SYSTOLIC – UPPER NO –	SYSTOLIC – LOWER NO –	HEART RATE	NOTE
MONDAY		AM	PM				
TUESDAY		AM	PM				
WEDNESDAY		AM	PM				
THURSDAY		AM	PM				
FRIDAY		AM	PM				
SATURDAY		AM	PM				
SUNDAY		AM	PM				

WEEK .... WEIGHT ....

DATE	TIME	AM	PM	SYSTOLIC – UPPER NO –	SYSTOLIC – LOWER NO –	HEART RATE	NOTE
MONDAY		AM	PM				
TUESDAY		AM	PM				
WEDNESDAY		AM	PM				
THURSDAY		AM	PM				
FRIDAY		AM	PM				
SATURDAY		AM	PM				
SUNDAY		AM	PM				

BLOOD
PRESSURE LOGBOOK

WEEK .... **WEIGHT** ....

DATE	TIME	AM	PM	SYSTOLIC - UPPER NO -	SYSTOLIC - LOWER NO -	HEART RATE	NOTE
MONDAY		AM	PM				
TUESDAY		AM	PM				
WEDNESDAY		AM	PM				
THURSDAY		AM	PM				
FRIDAY		AM	PM				
SATURDAY		AM	PM				
SUNDAY		AM	PM				

WEEK .... **WEIGHT** ....

DATE	TIME	AM	PM	SYSTOLIC - UPPER NO -	SYSTOLIC - LOWER NO -	HEART RATE	NOTE
MONDAY		AM	PM				
TUESDAY		AM	PM				
WEDNESDAY		AM	PM				
THURSDAY		AM	PM				
FRIDAY		AM	PM				
SATURDAY		AM	PM				
SUNDAY		AM	PM				

# BLOOD PRESSURE LOGBOOK

WEEK .... WEIGHT ....

DATE	TIME	AM	PM	SYSTOLIC – UPPER NO –	SYSTOLIC – LOWER NO –	HEART RATE	NOTE
MONDAY		AM	PM				
TUESDAY		AM	PM				
WEDNESDAY		AM	PM				
THURSDAY		AM	PM				
FRIDAY		AM	PM				
SATURDAY		AM	PM				
SUNDAY		AM	PM				

WEEK .... WEIGHT ....

DATE	TIME	AM	PM	SYSTOLIC – UPPER NO –	SYSTOLIC – LOWER NO –	HEART RATE	NOTE
MONDAY		AM	PM				
TUESDAY		AM	PM				
WEDNESDAY		AM	PM				
THURSDAY		AM	PM				
FRIDAY		AM	PM				
SATURDAY		AM	PM				
SUNDAY		AM	PM				

BLOOD
PRESSURE LOGBOOK

WEEK _______________________ WEIGHT _______________________

DATE	TIME	AM	PM	SYSTOLIC – UPPER NO –	SYSTOLIC – LOWER NO –	HEART RATE	NOTE
MONDAY		AM	PM				
TUESDAY		AM	PM				
WEDNESDAY		AM	PM				
THURSDAY		AM	PM				
FRIDAY		AM	PM				
SATURDAY		AM	PM				
SUNDAY		AM	PM				

WEEK _______________________ WEIGHT _______________________

DATE	TIME	AM	PM	SYSTOLIC – UPPER NO –	SYSTOLIC – LOWER NO –	HEART RATE	NOTE
MONDAY		AM	PM				
TUESDAY		AM	PM				
WEDNESDAY		AM	PM				
THURSDAY		AM	PM				
FRIDAY		AM	PM				
SATURDAY		AM	PM				
SUNDAY		AM	PM				

BLOOD
PRESSURE LOGBOOK

WEEK .... **WEIGHT** ....

DATE	TIME	AM	PM	SYSTOLIC – UPPER NO –	SYSTOLIC – LOWER NO –	HEART RATE	NOTE
MONDAY		AM	PM				
TUESDAY		AM	PM				
WEDNESDAY		AM	PM				
THURSDAY		AM	PM				
FRIDAY		AM	PM				
SATURDAY		AM	PM				
SUNDAY		AM	PM				

WEEK .... **WEIGHT** ....

DATE	TIME	AM	PM	SYSTOLIC – UPPER NO –	SYSTOLIC – LOWER NO –	HEART RATE	NOTE
MONDAY		AM	PM				
TUESDAY		AM	PM				
WEDNESDAY		AM	PM				
THURSDAY		AM	PM				
FRIDAY		AM	PM				
SATURDAY		AM	PM				
SUNDAY		AM	PM				

BLOOD
PRESSURE LOGBOOK

WEEK .... **WEIGHT** ....

DATE	TIME	AM	PM	SYSTOLIC - UPPER NO -	SYSTOLIC - LOWER NO -	HEART RATE	NOTE
MONDAY		AM	PM				
TUESDAY		AM	PM				
WEDNESDAY		AM	PM				
THURSDAY		AM	PM				
FRIDAY		AM	PM				
SATURDAY		AM	PM				
SUNDAY		AM	PM				

WEEK .... **WEIGHT** ....

DATE	TIME	AM	PM	SYSTOLIC - UPPER NO -	SYSTOLIC - LOWER NO -	HEART RATE	NOTE
MONDAY		AM	PM				
TUESDAY		AM	PM				
WEDNESDAY		AM	PM				
THURSDAY		AM	PM				
FRIDAY		AM	PM				
SATURDAY		AM	PM				
SUNDAY		AM	PM				

BLOOD
PRESSURE LOGBOOK

WEEK .... **WEIGHT** ....

DATE	TIME	AM	PM	SYSTOLIC - UPPER NO -	SYSTOLIC - LOWER NO -	HEART RATE	NOTE
MONDAY		AM	PM				
TUESDAY		AM	PM				
WEDNESDAY		AM	PM				
THURSDAY		AM	PM				
FRIDAY		AM	PM				
SATURDAY		AM	PM				
SUNDAY		AM	PM				

WEEK .... **WEIGHT** ....

DATE	TIME	AM	PM	SYSTOLIC - UPPER NO -	SYSTOLIC - LOWER NO -	HEART RATE	NOTE
MONDAY		AM	PM				
TUESDAY		AM	PM				
WEDNESDAY		AM	PM				
THURSDAY		AM	PM				
FRIDAY		AM	PM				
SATURDAY		AM	PM				
SUNDAY		AM	PM				

BLOOD
PRESSURE LOGBOOK

WEEK .... WEIGHT ....

DATE	TIME	AM	PM	SYSTOLIC – UPPER NO –	SYSTOLIC – LOWER NO –	HEART RATE	NOTE
MONDAY		AM	PM				
TUESDAY		AM	PM				
WEDNESDAY		AM	PM				
THURSDAY		AM	PM				
FRIDAY		AM	PM				
SATURDAY		AM	PM				
SUNDAY		AM	PM				

WEEK .... WEIGHT ....

DATE	TIME	AM	PM	SYSTOLIC – UPPER NO –	SYSTOLIC – LOWER NO –	HEART RATE	NOTE
MONDAY		AM	PM				
TUESDAY		AM	PM				
WEDNESDAY		AM	PM				
THURSDAY		AM	PM				
FRIDAY		AM	PM				
SATURDAY		AM	PM				
SUNDAY		AM	PM				

BLOOD PRESSURE LOGBOOK

WEEK _______________________ WEIGHT _______________________

DATE	TIME	AM	PM	SYSTOLIC – UPPER NO –	SYSTOLIC – LOWER NO –	HEART RATE	NOTE
MONDAY		AM	PM				
TUESDAY		AM	PM				
WEDNESDAY		AM	PM				
THURSDAY		AM	PM				
FRIDAY		AM	PM				
SATURDAY		AM	PM				
SUNDAY		AM	PM				

WEEK _______________________ WEIGHT _______________________

DATE	TIME	AM	PM	SYSTOLIC – UPPER NO –	SYSTOLIC – LOWER NO –	HEART RATE	NOTE
MONDAY		AM	PM				
TUESDAY		AM	PM				
WEDNESDAY		AM	PM				
THURSDAY		AM	PM				
FRIDAY		AM	PM				
SATURDAY		AM	PM				
SUNDAY		AM	PM				

BLOOD
PRESSURE LOGBOOK

WEEK ______________________ WEIGHT ______________________

DATE	TIME	AM	PM	SYSTOLIC – UPPER NO –	SYSTOLIC – LOWER NO –	HEART RATE	NOTE
MONDAY		AM	PM				
TUESDAY		AM	PM				
WEDNESDAY		AM	PM				
THURSDAY		AM	PM				
FRIDAY		AM	PM				
SATURDAY		AM	PM				
SUNDAY		AM	PM				

WEEK ______________________ WEIGHT ______________________

DATE	TIME	AM	PM	SYSTOLIC – UPPER NO –	SYSTOLIC – LOWER NO –	HEART RATE	NOTE
MONDAY		AM	PM				
TUESDAY		AM	PM				
WEDNESDAY		AM	PM				
THURSDAY		AM	PM				
FRIDAY		AM	PM				
SATURDAY		AM	PM				
SUNDAY		AM	PM				

BLOOD
PRESSURE LOGBOOK

WEEK .... **WEIGHT** ....

DATE	TIME	AM	PM	SYSTOLIC – UPPER NO –	SYSTOLIC – LOWER NO –	HEART RATE	NOTE
MONDAY		AM	PM				
TUESDAY		AM	PM				
WEDNESDAY		AM	PM				
THURSDAY		AM	PM				
FRIDAY		AM	PM				
SATURDAY		AM	PM				
SUNDAY		AM	PM				

WEEK .... **WEIGHT** ....

DATE	TIME	AM	PM	SYSTOLIC – UPPER NO –	SYSTOLIC – LOWER NO –	HEART RATE	NOTE
MONDAY		AM	PM				
TUESDAY		AM	PM				
WEDNESDAY		AM	PM				
THURSDAY		AM	PM				
FRIDAY		AM	PM				
SATURDAY		AM	PM				
SUNDAY		AM	PM				

BLOOD
PRESSURE LOGBOOK

WEEK .... **WEIGHT** ....

DATE	TIME	AM	PM	SYSTOLIC - UPPER NO -	SYSTOLIC - LOWER NO -	HEART RATE	NOTE
MONDAY		AM	PM				
TUESDAY		AM	PM				
WEDNESDAY		AM	PM				
THURSDAY		AM	PM				
FRIDAY		AM	PM				
SATURDAY		AM	PM				
SUNDAY		AM	PM				

WEEK .... **WEIGHT** ....

DATE	TIME	AM	PM	SYSTOLIC - UPPER NO -	SYSTOLIC - LOWER NO -	HEART RATE	NOTE
MONDAY		AM	PM				
TUESDAY		AM	PM				
WEDNESDAY		AM	PM				
THURSDAY		AM	PM				
FRIDAY		AM	PM				
SATURDAY		AM	PM				
SUNDAY		AM	PM				

BLOOD PRESSURE LOGBOOK

WEEK .... WEIGHT ....

DATE	TIME	AM	PM	SYSTOLIC - UPPER NO -	SYSTOLIC - LOWER NO -	HEART RATE	NOTE
MONDAY		AM	PM				
TUESDAY		AM	PM				
WEDNESDAY		AM	PM				
THURSDAY		AM	PM				
FRIDAY		AM	PM				
SATURDAY		AM	PM				
SUNDAY		AM	PM				

WEEK .... WEIGHT ....

DATE	TIME	AM	PM	SYSTOLIC - UPPER NO -	SYSTOLIC - LOWER NO -	HEART RATE	NOTE
MONDAY		AM	PM				
TUESDAY		AM	PM				
WEDNESDAY		AM	PM				
THURSDAY		AM	PM				
FRIDAY		AM	PM				
SATURDAY		AM	PM				
SUNDAY		AM	PM				

BLOOD
PRESSURE LOGBOOK

WEEK .... **WEIGHT** ....

DATE	TIME	AM	PM	SYSTOLIC - UPPER NO -	SYSTOLIC - LOWER NO -	HEART RATE	NOTE
MONDAY		AM	PM				
TUESDAY		AM	PM				
WEDNESDAY		AM	PM				
THURSDAY		AM	PM				
FRIDAY		AM	PM				
SATURDAY		AM	PM				
SUNDAY		AM	PM				

WEEK .... **WEIGHT** ....

DATE	TIME	AM	PM	SYSTOLIC - UPPER NO -	SYSTOLIC - LOWER NO -	HEART RATE	NOTE
MONDAY		AM	PM				
TUESDAY		AM	PM				
WEDNESDAY		AM	PM				
THURSDAY		AM	PM				
FRIDAY		AM	PRM				
SATURDAY		AM	PM				
SUNDAY		AM	PM				

BLOOD
PRESSURE LOGBOOK

WEEK .... **WEIGHT** ....

DATE	TIME	AM	PM	SYSTOLIC – UPPER NO –	SYSTOLIC – LOWER NO –	HEART RATE	NOTE
MONDAY		AM	PM				
TUESDAY		AM	PM				
WEDNESDAY		AM	PM				
THURSDAY		AM	PM				
FRIDAY		AM	PM				
SATURDAY		AM	PM				
SUNDAY		AM	PM				

WEEK .... **WEIGHT** ....

DATE	TIME	AM	PM	SYSTOLIC – UPPER NO –	SYSTOLIC – LOWER NO –	HEART RATE	NOTE
MONDAY		AM	PM				
TUESDAY		AM	PM				
WEDNESDAY		AM	PM				
THURSDAY		AM	PM				
FRIDAY		AM	PM				
SATURDAY		AM	PM				
SUNDAY		AM	PM				

BLOOD
PRESSURE LOGBOOK

WEEK .... **WEIGHT** ....

DATE	TIME	AM	PM	SYSTOLIC – UPPER NO –	SYSTOLIC – LOWER NO –	HEART RATE	NOTE
MONDAY		AM	PM				
TUESDAY		AM	PM				
WEDNESDAY		AM	PM				
THURSDAY		AM	PM				
FRIDAY		AM	PM				
SATURDAY		AM	PM				
SUNDAY		AM	PM				

WEEK .... **WEIGHT** ....

DATE	TIME	AM	PM	SYSTOLIC – UPPER NO –	SYSTOLIC – LOWER NO –	HEART RATE	NOTE
MONDAY		AM	PM				
TUESDAY		AM	PM				
WEDNESDAY		AM	PM				
THURSDAY		AM	PM				
FRIDAY		AM	PM				
SATURDAY		AM	PM				
SUNDAY		AM	PM				

BLOOD
PRESSURE LOGBOOK

WEEK _________________________ **WEIGHT** _____________________________

DATE	TIME	AM	PM	SYSTOLIC - UPPER NO -	SYSTOLIC - LOWER NO -	HEART RATE	NOTE
MONDAY		AM	PM				
TUESDAY		AM	PM				
WEDNESDAY		AM	PM				
THURSDAY		AM	PM				
FRIDAY		AM	PM				
SATURDAY		AM	PM				
SUNDAY		AM	PM				

WEEK _________________________ **WEIGHT** _____________________________

DATE	TIME	AM	PM	SYSTOLIC - UPPER NO -	SYSTOLIC - LOWER NO -	HEART RATE	NOTE
MONDAY		AM	PM				
TUESDAY		AM	PM				
WEDNESDAY		AM	PM				
THURSDAY		AM	PM				
FRIDAY		AM	PM				
SATURDAY		AM	PM				
SUNDAY		AM	PM				

BLOOD PRESSURE LOGBOOK

WEEK _______________________________ **WEIGHT** _______________________________

DATE	TIME	AM	PM	SYSTOLIC – UPPER NO –	SYSTOLIC – LOWER NO –	HEART RATE	NOTE
MONDAY		AM	PM				
TUESDAY		AM	PM				
WEDNESDAY		AM	PM				
THURSDAY		AM	PM				
FRIDAY		AM	PM				
SATURDAY		AM	PM				
SUNDAY		AM	PM				

WEEK _______________________________ **WEIGHT** _______________________________

DATE	TIME	AM	PM	SYSTOLIC – UPPER NO –	SYSTOLIC – LOWER NO –	HEART RATE	NOTE
MONDAY		AM	PM				
TUESDAY		AM	PM				
WEDNESDAY		AM	PM				
THURSDAY		AM	PM				
FRIDAY		AM	PM				
SATURDAY		AM	PM				
SUNDAY		AM	PM				

BLOOD
PRESSURE LOGBOOK

WEEK .... **WEIGHT** ....

DATE	TIME	AM	PM	SYSTOLIC – UPPER NO –	SYSTOLIC – LOWER NO –	HEART RATE	NOTE
MONDAY		AM	PM				
TUESDAY		AM	PM				
WEDNESDAY		AM	PM				
THURSDAY		AM	PM				
FRIDAY		AM	PM				
SATURDAY		AM	PM				
SUNDAY		AM	PM				

WEEK .... **WEIGHT** ....

DATE	TIME	AM	PM	SYSTOLIC – UPPER NO –	SYSTOLIC – LOWER NO –	HEART RATE	NOTE
MONDAY		AM	PM				
TUESDAY		AM	PM				
WEDNESDAY		AM	PM				
THURSDAY		AM	PM				
FRIDAY		AM	PM				
SATURDAY		AM	PM				
SUNDAY		AM	PM				

BLOOD
PRESSURE LOGBOOK

WEEK .... **WEIGHT** ....

DATE	TIME	AM	PM	SYSTOLIC - UPPER NO -	SYSTOLIC - LOWER NO -	HEART RATE	NOTE
MONDAY		AM	PM				
TUESDAY		AM	PM				
WEDNESDAY		AM	PM				
THURSDAY		AM	PM				
FRIDAY		AM	PM				
SATURDAY		AM	PM				
SUNDAY		AM	PM				

WEEK .... **WEIGHT** ....

DATE	TIME	AM	PM	SYSTOLIC - UPPER NO -	SYSTOLIC - LOWER NO -	HEART RATE	NOTE
MONDAY		AM	PM				
TUESDAY		AM	PM				
WEDNESDAY		AM	PM				
THURSDAY		AM	PM				
FRIDAY		AM	PM				
SATURDAY		AM	PM				
SUNDAY		AM	PM				

BLOOD
PRESSURE LOGBOOK

WEEK ________________________   WEIGHT ________________________

DATE	TIME	AM	PM	SYSTOLIC – UPPER NO –	SYSTOLIC – LOWER NO –	HEART RATE	NOTE
MONDAY		AM	PM				
TUESDAY		AM	PM				
WEDNESDAY		AM	PM				
THURSDAY		AM	PM				
FRIDAY		AM	PM				
SATURDAY		AM	PM				
SUNDAY		AM	PM				

WEEK ________________________   WEIGHT ________________________

DATE	TIME	AM	PM	SYSTOLIC – UPPER NO –	SYSTOLIC – LOWER NO –	HEART RATE	NOTE
MONDAY		AM	PM				
TUESDAY		AM	PM				
WEDNESDAY		AM	PM				
THURSDAY		AM	PM				
FRIDAY		AM	PM				
SATURDAY		AM	PM				
SUNDAY		AM	PM				

BLOOD
PRESSURE LOGBOOK

WEEK ________________________ **WEIGHT** ________________________

DATE	TIME	AM	PM	SYSTOLIC – UPPER NO –	SYSTOLIC – LOWER NO –	HEART RATE	NOTE
MONDAY		AM	PM				
TUESDAY		AM	PM				
WEDNESDAY		AM	PM				
THURSDAY		AM	PM				
FRIDAY		AM	PM				
SATURDAY		AM	PM				
SUNDAY		AM	PM				

WEEK ________________________ **WEIGHT** ________________________

DATE	TIME	AM	PM	SYSTOLIC – UPPER NO –	SYSTOLIC – LOWER NO –	HEART RATE	NOTE
MONDAY		AM	PM				
TUESDAY		AM	PM				
WEDNESDAY		AM	PM				
THURSDAY		AM	PM				
FRIDAY		AM	PM				
SATURDAY		AM	PM				
SUNDAY		AM	PM				

BLOOD PRESSURE LOGBOOK

WEEK .... **WEIGHT** ....

DATE	TIME	AM	PM	SYSTOLIC – UPPER NO –	SYSTOLIC – LOWER NO –	HEART RATE	NOTE
MONDAY		AM	PM				
TUESDAY		AM	PM				
WEDNESDAY		AM	PM				
THURSDAY		AM	PM				
FRIDAY		AM	PM				
SATURDAY		AM	PM				
SUNDAY		AM	PM				

WEEK .... **WEIGHT** ....

DATE	TIME	AM	PM	SYSTOLIC – UPPER NO –	SYSTOLIC – LOWER NO –	HEART RATE	NOTE
MONDAY		AM	PM				
TUESDAY		AM	PM				
WEDNESDAY		AM	PM				
THURSDAY		AM	PM				
FRIDAY		AM	PM				
SATURDAY		AM	PM				
SUNDAY		AM	PM				

 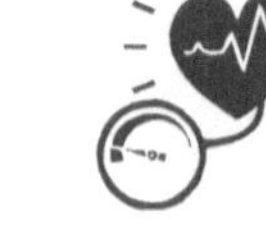

BLOOD PRESSURE LOGBOOK

WEEK ________________________________ **WEIGHT** ________________________________

DATE	TIME	AM	PM	SYSTOLIC – UPPER NO –	SYSTOLIC – LOWER NO –	HEART RATE	NOTE
MONDAY		AM	PM				
TUESDAY		AM	PM				
WEDNESDAY		AM	PM				
THURSDAY		AM	PM				
FRIDAY		AM	PM				
SATURDAY		AM	PM				
SUNDAY		AM	PM				

WEEK ________________________________ **WEIGHT** ________________________________

DATE	TIME	AM	PM	SYSTOLIC – UPPER NO –	SYSTOLIC – LOWER NO –	HEART RATE	NOTE
MONDAY		AM	PM				
TUESDAY		AM	PM				
WEDNESDAY		AM	PM				
THURSDAY		AM	PM				
FRIDAY		AM	PM				
SATURDAY		AM	PM				
SUNDAY		AM	PM				

BLOOD
PRESSURE LOGBOOK

WEEK .... WEIGHT ....

DATE	TIME	AM	PM	SYSTOLIC – UPPER NO –	SYSTOLIC – LOWER NO –	HEART RATE	NOTE
MONDAY		AM	PM				
TUESDAY		AM	PM				
WEDNESDAY		AM	PM				
THURSDAY		AM	PM				
FRIDAY		AM	PM				
SATURDAY		AM	PM				
SUNDAY		AM	PM				

WEEK .... WEIGHT ....

DATE	TIME	AM	PM	SYSTOLIC – UPPER NO –	SYSTOLIC – LOWER NO –	HEART RATE	NOTE
MONDAY		AM	PM				
TUESDAY		AM	PM				
WEDNESDAY		AM	PM				
THURSDAY		AM	PM				
FRIDAY		AM	PM				
SATURDAY		AM	PM				
SUNDAY		AM	PM				

BLOOD
PRESSURE LOGBOOK

WEEK ______________________________ **WEIGHT** ______________________________

DATE	TIME	AM	PM	SYSTOLIC – UPPER NO –	SYSTOLIC – LOWER NO –	HEART RATE	NOTE
MONDAY		AM	PM				
TUESDAY		AM	PM				
WEDNESDAY		AM	PM				
THURSDAY		AM	PM				
FRIDAY		AM	PM				
SATURDAY		AM	PM				
SUNDAY		AM	PM				

WEEK ______________________________ **WEIGHT** ______________________________

DATE	TIME	AM	PM	SYSTOLIC – UPPER NO –	SYSTOLIC – LOWER NO –	HEART RATE	NOTE
MONDAY		AM	PM				
TUESDAY		AM	PM				
WEDNESDAY		AM	PM				
THURSDAY		AM	PM				
FRIDAY		AM	PM				
SATURDAY		AM	PM				
SUNDAY		AM	PM				

BLOOD
PRESSURE LOGBOOK

WEEK .... **WEIGHT** ....

DATE	TIME	AM	PM	SYSTOLIC – UPPER NO –	SYSTOLIC – LOWER NO –	HEART RATE	NOTE
MONDAY		AM	PM				
TUESDAY		AM	PM				
WEDNESDAY		AM	PM				
THURSDAY		AM	PM				
FRIDAY		AM	PM				
SATURDAY		AM	PM				
SUNDAY		AM	PM				

WEEK .... **WEIGHT** ....

DATE	TIME	AM	PM	SYSTOLIC – UPPER NO –	SYSTOLIC – LOWER NO –	HEART RATE	NOTE
MONDAY		AM	PM				
TUESDAY		AM	PM				
WEDNESDAY		AM	PM				
THURSDAY		AM	PM				
FRIDAY		AM	PRESS				
SATURDAY		AM	PM				
SUNDAY		AM	PM				

BLOOD
PRESSURE LOGBOOK

WEEK _______________________________________ **WEIGHT** _______________________________________

DATE	TIME	AM	PM	SYSTOLIC – UPPER NO –	SYSTOLIC – LOWER NO –	HEART RATE	NOTE
MONDAY		AM	PM				
TUESDAY		AM	PM				
WEDNESDAY		AM	PM				
THURSDAY		AM	PM				
FRIDAY		AM	PM				
SATURDAY		AM	PM				
SUNDAY		AM	PM				

WEEK _______________________________________ **WEIGHT** _______________________________________

DATE	TIME	AM	PM	SYSTOLIC – UPPER NO –	SYSTOLIC – LOWER NO –	HEART RATE	NOTE
MONDAY		AM	PM				
TUESDAY		AM	PM				
WEDNESDAY		AM	PM				
THURSDAY		AM	PM				
FRIDAY		AM	PM				
SATURDAY		AM	PM				
SUNDAY		AM	PM				

BLOOD
PRESSURE LOGBOOK

WEEK ________________________ **WEIGHT** ________________________

DATE	TIME	AM	PM	SYSTOLIC – UPPER NO –	SYSTOLIC – LOWER NO –	HEART RATE	NOTE
MONDAY		AM	PM				
TUESDAY		AM	PM				
WEDNESDAY		AM	PM				
THURSDAY		AM	PM				
FRIDAY		AM	PM				
SATURDAY		AM	PM				
SUNDAY		AM	PM				

WEEK ________________________ **WEIGHT** ________________________

DATE	TIME	AM	PM	SYSTOLIC – UPPER NO –	SYSTOLIC – LOWER NO –	HEART RATE	NOTE
MONDAY		AM	PM				
TUESDAY		AM	PM				
WEDNESDAY		AM	PM				
THURSDAY		AM	PM				
FRIDAY		AM	PM				
SATURDAY		AM	PM				
SUNDAY		AM	PM				

BLOOD
PRESSURE LOGBOOK

WEEK ______________________ **WEIGHT** ______________________

DATE	TIME	AM	PM	SYSTOLIC – UPPER NO –	SYSTOLIC – LOWER NO –	HEART RATE	NOTE
MONDAY		AM	PM				
TUESDAY		AM	PM				
WEDNESDAY		AM	PM				
THURSDAY		AM	PM				
FRIDAY		AM	PM				
SATURDAY		AM	PM				
SUNDAY		AM	PM				

WEEK ______________________ **WEIGHT** ______________________

DATE	TIME	AM	PM	SYSTOLIC – UPPER NO –	SYSTOLIC – LOWER NO –	HEART RATE	NOTE
MONDAY		AM	PM				
TUESDAY		AM	PM				
WEDNESDAY		AM	PM				
THURSDAY		AM	PM				
FRIDAY		AM	PM				
SATURDAY		AM	PM				
SUNDAY		AM	PM				

BLOOD
PRESSURE LOGBOOK

WEEK .... **WEIGHT** ....

DATE	TIME	AM	PM	SYSTOLIC - UPPER NO -	SYSTOLIC - LOWER NO -	HEART RATE	NOTE
MONDAY		AM	PM				
TUESDAY		AM	PM				
WEDNESDAY		AM	PM				
THURSDAY		AM	PM				
FRIDAY		AM	PM				
SATURDAY		AM	PM				
SUNDAY		AM	PM				

WEEK .... **WEIGHT** ....

DATE	TIME	AM	PM	SYSTOLIC - UPPER NO -	SYSTOLIC - LOWER NO -	HEART RATE	NOTE
MONDAY		AM	PM				
TUESDAY		AM	PM				
WEDNESDAY		AM	PM				
THURSDAY		AM	PM				
FRIDAY		AM	PRM				
SATURDAY		AM	PM				
SUNDAY		AM	PM				

BLOOD
PRESSURE LOGBOOK

WEEK .... **WEIGHT** ....

DATE	TIME	AM	PM	SYSTOLIC – UPPER NO –	SYSTOLIC – LOWER NO –	HEART RATE	NOTE
MONDAY		AM	PM				
TUESDAY		AM	PM				
WEDNESDAY		AM	PM				
THURSDAY		AM	PM				
FRIDAY		AM	PM				
SATURDAY		AM	PM				
SUNDAY		AM	PM				

WEEK .... **WEIGHT** ....

DATE	TIME	AM	PM	SYSTOLIC – UPPER NO –	SYSTOLIC – LOWER NO –	HEART RATE	NOTE
MONDAY		AM	PM				
TUESDAY		AM	PM				
WEDNESDAY		AM	PM				
THURSDAY		AM	PM				
FRIDAY		AM	PM				
SATURDAY		AM	PM				
SUNDAY		AM	PM				

BLOOD PRESSURE LOGBOOK

WEEK .... **WEIGHT** ....

DATE	TIME	AM	PM	SYSTOLIC – UPPER NO –	SYSTOLIC – LOWER NO –	HEART RATE	NOTE
MONDAY		AM	PM				
TUESDAY		AM	PM				
WEDNESDAY		AM	PM				
THURSDAY		AM	PM				
FRIDAY		AM	PM				
SATURDAY		AM	PM				
SUNDAY		AM	PM				

WEEK .... **WEIGHT** ....

DATE	TIME	AM	PM	SYSTOLIC – UPPER NO –	SYSTOLIC – LOWER NO –	HEART RATE	NOTE
MONDAY		AM	PM				
TUESDAY		AM	PM				
WEDNESDAY		AM	PM				
THURSDAY		AM	PM				
FRIDAY		AM	PM				
SATURDAY		AM	PM				
SUNDAY		AM	PM				

BLOOD PRESSURE LOGBOOK

WEEK ________________________   WEIGHT ________________________

DATE	TIME	AM	PM	SYSTOLIC – UPPER NO –	SYSTOLIC – LOWER NO –	HEART RATE	NOTE
MONDAY		AM	PM				
TUESDAY		AM	PM				
WEDNESDAY		AM	PM				
THURSDAY		AM	PM				
FRIDAY		AM	PM				
SATURDAY		AM	PM				
SUNDAY		AM	PM				

WEEK ________________________   WEIGHT ________________________

DATE	TIME	AM	PM	SYSTOLIC – UPPER NO –	SYSTOLIC – LOWER NO –	HEART RATE	NOTE
MONDAY		AM	PM				
TUESDAY		AM	PM				
WEDNESDAY		AM	PM				
THURSDAY		AM	PM				
FRIDAY		AM	PM				
SATURDAY		AM	PM				
SUNDAY		AM	PM				

BLOOD
PRESSURE LOGBOOK

WEEK .... WEIGHT ....

DATE	TIME	AM	PM	SYSTOLIC - UPPER NO -	SYSTOLIC - LOWER NO -	HEART RATE	NOTE
MONDAY		AM	PM				
TUESDAY		AM	PM				
WEDNESDAY		AM	PM				
THURSDAY		AM	PM				
FRIDAY		AM	PM				
SATURDAY		AM	PM				
SUNDAY		AM	PM				

WEEK .... WEIGHT ....

DATE	TIME	AM	PM	SYSTOLIC - UPPER NO -	SYSTOLIC - LOWER NO -	HEART RATE	NOTE
MONDAY		AM	PM				
TUESDAY		AM	PM				
WEDNESDAY		AM	PM				
THURSDAY		AM	PM				
FRIDAY		AM	PRM				
SATURDAY		AM	PM				
SUNDAY		AM	PM				

BLOOD
PRESSURE LOGBOOK

WEEK .... **WEIGHT** ....

DATE	TIME	AM	PM	SYSTOLIC – UPPER NO –	SYSTOLIC – LOWER NO –	HEART RATE	NOTE
MONDAY		AM	PM				
TUESDAY		AM	PM				
WEDNESDAY		AM	PM				
THURSDAY		AM	PM				
FRIDAY		AM	PM				
SATURDAY		AM	PM				
SUNDAY		AM	PM				

WEEK .... **WEIGHT** ....

DATE	TIME	AM	PM	SYSTOLIC – UPPER NO –	SYSTOLIC – LOWER NO –	HEART RATE	NOTE
MONDAY		AM	PM				
TUESDAY		AM	PM				
WEDNESDAY		AM	PM				
THURSDAY		AM	PM				
FRIDAY		AM	PM				
SATURDAY		AM	PM				
SUNDAY		AM	PM				

BLOOD PRESSURE LOGBOOK

WEEK _________________________ WEIGHT _________________________

DATE	TIME	AM	PM	SYSTOLIC - UPPER NO -	SYSTOLIC - LOWER NO -	HEART RATE	NOTE
MONDAY		AM	PM				
TUESDAY		AM	PM				
WEDNESDAY		AM	PM				
THURSDAY		AM	PM				
FRIDAY		AM	PM				
SATURDAY		AM	PM				
SUNDAY		AM	PM				

WEEK _________________________ WEIGHT _________________________

DATE	TIME	AM	PM	SYSTOLIC - UPPER NO -	SYSTOLIC - LOWER NO -	HEART RATE	NOTE
MONDAY		AM	PM				
TUESDAY		AM	PM				
WEDNESDAY		AM	PM				
THURSDAY		AM	PM				
FRIDAY		AM	PM				
SATURDAY		AM	PM				
SUNDAY		AM	PM				

# BLOOD PRESSURE LOGBOOK

WEEK .... **WEIGHT** ....

DATE	TIME	AM	PM	SYSTOLIC – UPPER NO –	SYSTOLIC – LOWER NO –	HEART RATE	NOTE
MONDAY		AM	PM				
TUESDAY		AM	PM				
WEDNESDAY		AM	PM				
THURSDAY		AM	PM				
FRIDAY		AM	PM				
SATURDAY		AM	PM				
SUNDAY		AM	PM				

WEEK .... **WEIGHT** ....

DATE	TIME	AM	PM	SYSTOLIC – UPPER NO –	SYSTOLIC – LOWER NO –	HEART RATE	NOTE
MONDAY		AM	PM				
TUESDAY		AM	PM				
WEDNESDAY		AM	PM				
THURSDAY		AM	PM				
FRIDAY		AM	PM				
SATURDAY		AM	PM				
SUNDAY		AM	PM				

BLOOD PRESSURE LOGBOOK

WEEK .... WEIGHT ....

DATE	TIME	AM	PM	SYSTOLIC – UPPER NO –	SYSTOLIC – LOWER NO –	HEART RATE	NOTE
MONDAY		AM	PM				
TUESDAY		AM	PM				
WEDNESDAY		AM	PM				
THURSDAY		AM	PM				
FRIDAY		AM	PM				
SATURDAY		AM	PM				
SUNDAY		AM	PM				

WEEK .... WEIGHT ....

DATE	TIME	AM	PM	SYSTOLIC – UPPER NO –	SYSTOLIC – LOWER NO –	HEART RATE	NOTE
MONDAY		AM	PM				
TUESDAY		AM	PM				
WEDNESDAY		AM	PM				
THURSDAY		AM	PM				
FRIDAY		AM	PM				
SATURDAY		AM	PM				
SUNDAY		AM	PM				

BLOOD
PRESSURE LOGBOOK

WEEK .... **WEIGHT** ....

DATE	TIME	AM	PM	SYSTOLIC – UPPER NO –	SYSTOLIC – LOWER NO –	HEART RATE	NOTE
MONDAY		AM	PM				
TUESDAY		AM	PM				
WEDNESDAY		AM	PM				
THURSDAY		AM	PM				
FRIDAY		AM	PM				
SATURDAY		AM	PM				
SUNDAY		AM	PM				

WEEK .... **WEIGHT** ....

DATE	TIME	AM	PM	SYSTOLIC – UPPER NO –	SYSTOLIC – LOWER NO –	HEART RATE	NOTE
MONDAY		AM	PM				
TUESDAY		AM	PM				
WEDNESDAY		AM	PM				
THURSDAY		AM	PM				
FRIDAY		AM	PM				
SATURDAY		AM	PM				
SUNDAY		AM	PM				

BLOOD
PRESSURE LOGBOOK

WEEK .... WEIGHT ....

DATE	TIME	AM	PM	SYSTOLIC – UPPER NO –	SYSTOLIC – LOWER NO –	HEART RATE	NOTE
MONDAY		AM	PM				
TUESDAY		AM	PM				
WEDNESDAY		AM	PM				
THURSDAY		AM	PM				
FRIDAY		AM	PM				
SATURDAY		AM	PM				
SUNDAY		AM	PM				

WEEK .... WEIGHT ....

DATE	TIME	AM	PM	SYSTOLIC – UPPER NO –	SYSTOLIC – LOWER NO –	HEART RATE	NOTE
MONDAY		AM	PM				
TUESDAY		AM	PM				
WEDNESDAY		AM	PM				
THURSDAY		AM	PM				
FRIDAY		AM	PM				
SATURDAY		AM	PM				
SUNDAY		AM	PM				

BLOOD PRESSURE LOGBOOK

WEEK ________________________   WEIGHT ________________________

DATE	TIME	AM	PM	SYSTOLIC – UPPER NO –	SYSTOLIC – LOWER NO –	HEART RATE	NOTE
MONDAY		AM	PM				
TUESDAY		AM	PM				
WEDNESDAY		AM	PM				
THURSDAY		AM	PM				
FRIDAY		AM	PM				
SATURDAY		AM	PM				
SUNDAY		AM	PM				

WEEK ________________________   WEIGHT ________________________

DATE	TIME	AM	PM	SYSTOLIC – UPPER NO –	SYSTOLIC – LOWER NO –	HEART RATE	NOTE
MONDAY		AM	PM				
TUESDAY		AM	PM				
WEDNESDAY		AM	PM				
THURSDAY		AM	PM				
FRIDAY		AM	PRM				
SATURDAY		AM	PM				
SUNDAY		AM	PM				

BLOOD
PRESSURE LOGBOOK

WEEK .... WEIGHT ....

DATE	TIME	AM	PM	SYSTOLIC - UPPER NO -	SYSTOLIC - LOWER NO -	HEART RATE	NOTE
MONDAY		AM	PM				
TUESDAY		AM	PM				
WEDNESDAY		AM	PM				
THURSDAY		AM	PM				
FRIDAY		AM	PM				
SATURDAY		AM	PM				
SUNDAY		AM	PM				

WEEK .... WEIGHT ....

DATE	TIME	AM	PM	SYSTOLIC - UPPER NO -	SYSTOLIC - LOWER NO -	HEART RATE	NOTE
MONDAY		AM	PM				
TUESDAY		AM	PM				
WEDNESDAY		AM	PM				
THURSDAY		AM	PM				
FRIDAY		AM	PM				
SATURDAY		AM	PM				
SUNDAY		AM	PM				

BLOOD PRESSURE LOGBOOK

WEEK ____________________________ **WEIGHT** ____________________________

DATE	TIME	AM	PM	SYSTOLIC - UPPER NO -	SYSTOLIC - LOWER NO -	HEART RATE	NOTE
MONDAY		AM	PM				
TUESDAY		AM	PM				
WEDNESDAY		AM	PM				
THURSDAY		AM	PM				
FRIDAY		AM	PM				
SATURDAY		AM	PM				
SUNDAY		AM	PM				

WEEK ____________________________ **WEIGHT** ____________________________

DATE	TIME	AM	PM	SYSTOLIC - UPPER NO -	SYSTOLIC - LOWER NO -	HEART RATE	NOTE
MONDAY		AM	PM				
TUESDAY		AM	PM				
WEDNESDAY		AM	PM				
THURSDAY		AM	PM				
FRIDAY		AM	PM				
SATURDAY		AM	PM				
SUNDAY		AM	PM				

BLOOD
PRESSURE LOGBOOK

WEEK ________________________   WEIGHT ________________________

DATE	TIME	AM	PM	SYSTOLIC – UPPER NO –	SYSTOLIC – LOWER NO –	HEART RATE	NOTE
MONDAY		AM	PM				
TUESDAY		AM	PM				
WEDNESDAY		AM	PM				
THURSDAY		AM	PM				
FRIDAY		AM	PM				
SATURDAY		AM	PM				
SUNDAY		AM	PM				

WEEK ________________________   WEIGHT ________________________

DATE	TIME	AM	PM	SYSTOLIC – UPPER NO –	SYSTOLIC – LOWER NO –	HEART RATE	NOTE
MONDAY		AM	PM				
TUESDAY		AM	PM				
WEDNESDAY		AM	PM				
THURSDAY		AM	PM				
FRIDAY		AM	PM				
SATURDAY		AM	PM				
SUNDAY		AM	PM				

BLOOD
PRESSURE LOGBOOK

WEEK .... **WEIGHT** ....

DATE	TIME	AM	PM	SYSTOLIC – UPPER NO –	SYSTOLIC – LOWER NO –	HEART RATE	NOTE
MONDAY		AM	PM				
TUESDAY		AM	PM				
WEDNESDAY		AM	PM				
THURSDAY		AM	PM				
FRIDAY		AM	PM				
SATURDAY		AM	PM				
SUNDAY		AM	PM				

WEEK .... **WEIGHT** ....

DATE	TIME	AM	PM	SYSTOLIC – UPPER NO –	SYSTOLIC – LOWER NO –	HEART RATE	NOTE
MONDAY		AM	PM				
TUESDAY		AM	PM				
WEDNESDAY		AM	PM				
THURSDAY		AM	PM				
FRIDAY		AM	PM				
SATURDAY		AM	PM				
SUNDAY		AM	PM				

BLOOD
PRESSURE LOGBOOK

WEEK ....   WEIGHT ....

DATE	TIME	AM	PM	SYSTOLIC - UPPER NO -	SYSTOLIC - LOWER NO -	HEART RATE	NOTE
MONDAY		AM	PM				
TUESDAY		AM	PM				
WEDNESDAY		AM	PM				
THURSDAY		AM	PM				
FRIDAY		AM	PM				
SATURDAY		AM	PM				
SUNDAY		AM	PM				

WEEK ....   WEIGHT ....

DATE	TIME	AM	PM	SYSTOLIC - UPPER NO -	SYSTOLIC - LOWER NO -	HEART RATE	NOTE
MONDAY		AM	PM				
TUESDAY		AM	PM				
WEDNESDAY		AM	PM				
THURSDAY		AM	PM				
FRIDAY		AM	PM				
SATURDAY		AM	PM				
SUNDAY		AM	PM				

BLOOD
PRESSURE LOGBOOK

WEEK .... **WEIGHT** ....

DATE	TIME	AM	PM	SYSTOLIC – UPPER NO –	SYSTOLIC – LOWER NO –	HEART RATE	NOTE
MONDAY		AM	PM				
TUESDAY		AM	PM				
WEDNESDAY		AM	PM				
THURSDAY		AM	PM				
FRIDAY		AM	PM				
SATURDAY		AM	PM				
SUNDAY		AM	PM				

WEEK .... **WEIGHT** ....

DATE	TIME	AM	PM	SYSTOLIC – UPPER NO –	SYSTOLIC – LOWER NO –	HEART RATE	NOTE
MONDAY		AM	PM				
TUESDAY		AM	PM				
WEDNESDAY		AM	PM				
THURSDAY		AM	PM				
FRIDAY		AM	PM				
SATURDAY		AM	PM				
SUNDAY		AM	PM				

BLOOD PRESSURE LOGBOOK

WEEK .... **WEIGHT** ....

DATE	TIME	AM	PM	SYSTOLIC – UPPER NO –	SYSTOLIC – LOWER NO –	HEART RATE	NOTE
MONDAY		AM	PM				
TUESDAY		AM	PM				
WEDNESDAY		AM	PM				
THURSDAY		AM	PM				
FRIDAY		AM	PM				
SATURDAY		AM	PM				
SUNDAY		AM	PM				

WEEK .... **WEIGHT** ....

DATE	TIME	AM	PM	SYSTOLIC – UPPER NO –	SYSTOLIC – LOWER NO –	HEART RATE	NOTE
MONDAY		AM	PM				
TUESDAY		AM	PM				
WEDNESDAY		AM	PM				
THURSDAY		AM	PM				
FRIDAY		AM	PM				
SATURDAY		AM	PM				
SUNDAY		AM	PM				

BLOOD
PRESSURE LOGBOOK

WEEK .... **WEIGHT** ....

DATE	TIME	AM	PM	SYSTOLIC ~ UPPER NO ~	SYSTOLIC ~ LOWER NO ~	HEART RATE	NOTE
MONDAY		AM	PM				
TUESDAY		AM	PM				
WEDNESDAY		AM	PM				
THURSDAY		AM	PM				
FRIDAY		AM	PM				
SATURDAY		AM	PM				
SUNDAY		AM	PM				

WEEK .... **WEIGHT** ....

DATE	TIME	AM	PM	SYSTOLIC ~ UPPER NO ~	SYSTOLIC ~ LOWER NO ~	HEART RATE	NOTE
MONDAY		AM	PM				
TUESDAY		AM	PM				
WEDNESDAY		AM	PM				
THURSDAY		AM	PM				
FRIDAY		AM	PM				
SATURDAY		AM	PM				
SUNDAY		AM	PM				

BLOOD
PRESSURE LOGBOOK

WEEK _________________________________ **WEIGHT** _________________________________

DATE	TIME	AM	PM	SYSTOLIC – UPPER NO –	SYSTOLIC – LOWER NO –	HEART RATE	NOTE
MONDAY		AM	PM				
TUESDAY		AM	PM				
WEDNESDAY		AM	PM				
THURSDAY		AM	PM				
FRIDAY		AM	PM				
SATURDAY		AM	PM				
SUNDAY		AM	PM				

WEEK _________________________________ **WEIGHT** _________________________________

DATE	TIME	AM	PM	SYSTOLIC – UPPER NO –	SYSTOLIC – LOWER NO –	HEART RATE	NOTE
MONDAY		AM	PM				
TUESDAY		AM	PM				
WEDNESDAY		AM	PM				
THURSDAY		AM	PM				
FRIDAY		AM	PM				
SATURDAY		AM	PM				
SUNDAY		AM	PM				

BLOOD
PRESSURE LOGBOOK

WEEK .... WEIGHT ....

DATE	TIME	AM	PM	SYSTOLIC – UPPER NO –	SYSTOLIC – LOWER NO –	HEART RATE	NOTE
MONDAY		AM	PM				
TUESDAY		AM	PM				
WEDNESDAY		AM	PM				
THURSDAY		AM	PM				
FRIDAY		AM	PM				
SATURDAY		AM	PM				
SUNDAY		AM	PM				

WEEK .... WEIGHT ....

DATE	TIME	AM	PM	SYSTOLIC – UPPER NO –	SYSTOLIC – LOWER NO –	HEART RATE	NOTE
MONDAY		AM	PM				
TUESDAY		AM	PM				
WEDNESDAY		AM	PM				
THURSDAY		AM	PM				
FRIDAY		AM	PRM				
SATURDAY		AM	PM				
SUNDAY		AM	PM				

BLOOD
PRESSURE LOGBOOK

WEEK _______________________ WEIGHT _______________________

DATE	TIME	AM	PM	SYSTOLIC – UPPER NO –	SYSTOLIC – LOWER NO –	HEART RATE	NOTE
MONDAY		AM	PM				
TUESDAY		AM	PM				
WEDNESDAY		AM	PM				
THURSDAY		AM	PM				
FRIDAY		AM	PM				
SATURDAY		AM	PM				
SUNDAY		AM	PM				

WEEK _______________________ WEIGHT _______________________

DATE	TIME	AM	PM	SYSTOLIC – UPPER NO –	SYSTOLIC – LOWER NO –	HEART RATE	NOTE
MONDAY		AM	PM				
TUESDAY		AM	PM				
WEDNESDAY		AM	PM				
THURSDAY		AM	PM				
FRIDAY		AM	PM				
SATURDAY		AM	PM				
SUNDAY		AM	PM				

BLOOD
PRESSURE LOGBOOK

WEEK .... **WEIGHT** ....

DATE	TIME	AM	PM	SYSTOLIC – UPPER NO –	SYSTOLIC – LOWER NO –	HEART RATE	NOTE
MONDAY		AM	PM				
TUESDAY		AM	PM				
WEDNESDAY		AM	PM				
THURSDAY		AM	PM				
FRIDAY		AM	PM				
SATURDAY		AM	PM				
SUNDAY		AM	PM				

WEEK .... **WEIGHT** ....

DATE	TIME	AM	PM	SYSTOLIC – UPPER NO –	SYSTOLIC – LOWER NO –	HEART RATE	NOTE
MONDAY		AM	PM				
TUESDAY		AM	PM				
WEDNESDAY		AM	PM				
THURSDAY		AM	PM				
FRIDAY		AM	PM				
SATURDAY		AM	PM				
SUNDAY		AM	PM				

BLOOD PRESSURE LOGBOOK

WEEK .... WEIGHT ....

DATE	TIME	AM	PM	SYSTOLIC - UPPER NO -	SYSTOLIC - LOWER NO -	HEART RATE	NOTE
MONDAY		AM	PM				
TUESDAY		AM	PM				
WEDNESDAY		AM	PM				
THURSDAY		AM	PM				
FRIDAY		AM	PM				
SATURDAY		AM	PM				
SUNDAY		AM	PM				

WEEK .... WEIGHT ....

DATE	TIME	AM	PM	SYSTOLIC - UPPER NO -	SYSTOLIC - LOWER NO -	HEART RATE	NOTE
MONDAY		AM	PM				
TUESDAY		AM	PM				
WEDNESDAY		AM	PM				
THURSDAY		AM	PM				
FRIDAY		AM	PM				
SATURDAY		AM	PM				
SUNDAY		AM	PM				

BLOOD
PRESSURE LOGBOOK

WEEK ________________________________ **WEIGHT** ________________________________

DATE	TIME	AM	PM	SYSTOLIC - UPPER NO -	SYSTOLIC - LOWER NO -	HEART RATE	NOTE
MONDAY		AM	PM				
TUESDAY		AM	PM				
WEDNESDAY		AM	PM				
THURSDAY		AM	PM				
FRIDAY		AM	PM				
SATURDAY		AM	PM				
SUNDAY		AM	PM				

WEEK ________________________________ **WEIGHT** ________________________________

DATE	TIME	AM	PM	SYSTOLIC - UPPER NO -	SYSTOLIC - LOWER NO -	HEART RATE	NOTE
MONDAY		AM	PM				
TUESDAY		AM	PM				
WEDNESDAY		AM	PM				
THURSDAY		AM	PM				
FRIDAY		AM	PM				
SATURDAY		AM	PM				
SUNDAY		AM	PM				

BLOOD PRESSURE LOGBOOK

WEEK .... **WEIGHT** ....

DATE	TIME	AM	PM	SYSTOLIC – UPPER NO –	SYSTOLIC – LOWER NO –	HEART RATE	NOTE
MONDAY		AM	PM				
TUESDAY		AM	PM				
WEDNESDAY		AM	PM				
THURSDAY		AM	PM				
FRIDAY		AM	PM				
SATURDAY		AM	PM				
SUNDAY		AM	PM				

WEEK .... **WEIGHT** ....

DATE	TIME	AM	PM	SYSTOLIC – UPPER NO –	SYSTOLIC – LOWER NO –	HEART RATE	NOTE
MONDAY		AM	PM				
TUESDAY		AM	PM				
WEDNESDAY		AM	PM				
THURSDAY		AM	PM				
FRIDAY		AM	PM				
SATURDAY		AM	PM				
SUNDAY		AM	PM				

BLOOD PRESSURE LOGBOOK

WEEK _______________________________ **WEIGHT** _______________________________

DATE	TIME	AM	PM	SYSTOLIC – UPPER NO –	SYSTOLIC – LOWER NO –	HEART RATE	NOTE
MONDAY		AM	PM				
TUESDAY		AM	PM				
WEDNESDAY		AM	PM				
THURSDAY		AM	PM				
FRIDAY		AM	PM				
SATURDAY		AM	PM				
SUNDAY		AM	PM				

WEEK _______________________________ **WEIGHT** _______________________________

DATE	TIME	AM	PM	SYSTOLIC – UPPER NO –	SYSTOLIC – LOWER NO –	HEART RATE	NOTE
MONDAY		AM	PM				
TUESDAY		AM	PM				
WEDNESDAY		AM	PM				
THURSDAY		AM	PM				
FRIDAY		AM	PM				
SATURDAY		AM	PM				
SUNDAY		AM	PM				

BLOOD
PRESSURE LOGBOOK

WEEK .... WEIGHT ....

DATE	TIME	AM	PM	SYSTOLIC – UPPER NO –	SYSTOLIC – LOWER NO –	HEART RATE	NOTE
MONDAY		AM	PM				
TUESDAY		AM	PM				
WEDNESDAY		AM	PM				
THURSDAY		AM	PM				
FRIDAY		AM	PM				
SATURDAY		AM	PM				
SUNDAY		AM	PM				

WEEK .... WEIGHT ....

DATE	TIME	AM	PM	SYSTOLIC – UPPER NO –	SYSTOLIC – LOWER NO –	HEART RATE	NOTE
MONDAY		AM	PM				
TUESDAY		AM	PM				
WEDNESDAY		AM	PM				
THURSDAY		AM	PM				
FRIDAY		AM	PM				
SATURDAY		AM	PM				
SUNDAY		AM	PM				

BLOOD
PRESSURE LOGBOOK

WEEK ______________________________ **WEIGHT** ______________________________

DATE	TIME	AM	PM	SYSTOLIC – UPPER NO –	SYSTOLIC – LOWER NO –	HEART RATE	NOTE
MONDAY		AM	PM				
TUESDAY		AM	PM				
WEDNESDAY		AM	PM				
THURSDAY		AM	PM				
FRIDAY		AM	PM				
SATURDAY		AM	PM				
SUNDAY		AM	PM				

WEEK ______________________________ **WEIGHT** ______________________________

DATE	TIME	AM	PM	SYSTOLIC – UPPER NO –	SYSTOLIC – LOWER NO –	HEART RATE	NOTE
MONDAY		AM	PM				
TUESDAY		AM	PM				
WEDNESDAY		AM	PM				
THURSDAY		AM	PM				
FRIDAY		AM	PM				
SATURDAY		AM	PM				
SUNDAY		AM	PM				

BLOOD PRESSURE LOGBOOK

WEEK .... **WEIGHT** ....

DATE	TIME	AM	PM	SYSTOLIC – UPPER NO –	SYSTOLIC – LOWER NO –	HEART RATE	NOTE
MONDAY		AM	PM				
TUESDAY		AM	PM				
WEDNESDAY		AM	PM				
THURSDAY		AM	PM				
FRIDAY		AM	PM				
SATURDAY		AM	PM				
SUNDAY		AM	PM				

WEEK .... **WEIGHT** ....

DATE	TIME	AM	PM	SYSTOLIC – UPPER NO –	SYSTOLIC – LOWER NO –	HEART RATE	NOTE
MONDAY		AM	PM				
TUESDAY		AM	PM				
WEDNESDAY		AM	PM				
THURSDAY		AM	PM				
FRIDAY		AM	PM				
SATURDAY		AM	PM				
SUNDAY		AM	PM				

BLOOD
PRESSURE LOGBOOK

WEEK _______________________________ **WEIGHT** _______________________________

DATE	TIME	AM	PM	SYSTOLIC - UPPER NO -	SYSTOLIC - LOWER NO -	HEART RATE	NOTE
MONDAY		AM	PM				
TUESDAY		AM	PM				
WEDNESDAY		AM	PM				
THURSDAY		AM	PM				
FRIDAY		AM	PM				
SATURDAY		AM	PM				
SUNDAY		AM	PM				

WEEK _______________________________ **WEIGHT** _______________________________

DATE	TIME	AM	PM	SYSTOLIC - UPPER NO -	SYSTOLIC - LOWER NO -	HEART RATE	NOTE
MONDAY		AM	PM				
TUESDAY		AM	PM				
WEDNESDAY		AM	PM				
THURSDAY		AM	PM				
FRIDAY		AM	PM				
SATURDAY		AM	PM				
SUNDAY		AM	PM				

BLOOD
PRESSURE LOGBOOK

WEEK .... WEIGHT ....

DATE	TIME	AM	PM	SYSTOLIC – UPPER NO –	SYSTOLIC – LOWER NO –	HEART RATE	NOTE
MONDAY		AM	PM				
TUESDAY		AM	PM				
WEDNESDAY		AM	PM				
THURSDAY		AM	PM				
FRIDAY		AM	PM				
SATURDAY		AM	PM				
SUNDAY		AM	PM				

WEEK .... WEIGHT ....

DATE	TIME	AM	PM	SYSTOLIC – UPPER NO –	SYSTOLIC – LOWER NO –	HEART RATE	NOTE
MONDAY		AM	PM				
TUESDAY		AM	PM				
WEDNESDAY		AM	PM				
THURSDAY		AM	PM				
FRIDAY		AM	PM				
SATURDAY		AM	PM				
SUNDAY		AM	PM				

BLOOD
PRESSURE LOGBOOK

WEEK .... WEIGHT ....

DATE	TIME	AM	PM	SYSTOLIC – UPPER NO –	SYSTOLIC – LOWER NO –	HEART RATE	NOTE
MONDAY		AM	PM				
TUESDAY		AM	PM				
WEDNESDAY		AM	PM				
THURSDAY		AM	PM				
FRIDAY		AM	PM				
SATURDAY		AM	PM				
SUNDAY		AM	PM				

WEEK .... WEIGHT ....

DATE	TIME	AM	PM	SYSTOLIC – UPPER NO –	SYSTOLIC – LOWER NO –	HEART RATE	NOTE
MONDAY		AM	PM				
TUESDAY		AM	PM				
WEDNESDAY		AM	PM				
THURSDAY		AM	PM				
FRIDAY		AM	PM				
SATURDAY		AM	PM				
SUNDAY		AM	PM				

BLOOD
PRESSURE LOGBOOK

WEEK _________________________ WEIGHT _______________________________

DATE	TIME	AM	PM	SYSTOLIC - UPPER NO -	SYSTOLIC - LOWER NO -	HEART RATE	NOTE
MONDAY		AM	PM				
TUESDAY		AM	PM				
WEDNESDAY		AM	PM				
THURSDAY		AM	PM				
FRIDAY		AM	PM				
SATURDAY		AM	PM				
SUNDAY		AM	PM				

WEEK _________________________ WEIGHT _______________________________

DATE	TIME	AM	PM	SYSTOLIC - UPPER NO -	SYSTOLIC - LOWER NO -	HEART RATE	NOTE
MONDAY		AM	PM				
TUESDAY		AM	PM				
WEDNESDAY		AM	PM				
THURSDAY		AM	PM				
FRIDAY		AM	PM				
SATURDAY		AM	PM				
SUNDAY		AM	PM				

BLOOD
PRESSURE LOGBOOK

WEEK ___________________________ **WEIGHT** ___________________________

DATE	TIME	AM	PM	SYSTOLIC – UPPER NO –	SYSTOLIC – LOWER NO –	HEART RATE	NOTE
MONDAY		AM	PM				
TUESDAY		AM	PM				
WEDNESDAY		AM	PM				
THURSDAY		AM	PM				
FRIDAY		AM	PM				
SATURDAY		AM	PM				
SUNDAY		AM	PM				

WEEK ___________________________ **WEIGHT** ___________________________

DATE	TIME	AM	PM	SYSTOLIC – UPPER NO –	SYSTOLIC – LOWER NO –	HEART RATE	NOTE
MONDAY		AM	PM				
TUESDAY		AM	PM				
WEDNESDAY		AM	PM				
THURSDAY		AM	PM				
FRIDAY		AM	PM				
SATURDAY		AM	PM				
SUNDAY		AM	PM				

BLOOD
PRESSURE LOGBOOK

WEEK .... **WEIGHT** ....

DATE	TIME	AM	PM	SYSTOLIC – UPPER NO –	SYSTOLIC – LOWER NO –	HEART RATE	NOTE
MONDAY		AM	PM				
TUESDAY		AM	PM				
WEDNESDAY		AM	PM				
THURSDAY		AM	PM				
FRIDAY		AM	PM				
SATURDAY		AM	PM				
SUNDAY		AM	PM				

WEEK .... **WEIGHT** ....

DATE	TIME	AM	PM	SYSTOLIC – UPPER NO –	SYSTOLIC – LOWER NO –	HEART RATE	NOTE
MONDAY		AM	PM				
TUESDAY		AM	PM				
WEDNESDAY		AM	PM				
THURSDAY		AM	PM				
FRIDAY		AM	PM				
SATURDAY		AM	PM				
SUNDAY		AM	PM				

BLOOD
PRESSURE LOGBOOK

WEEK _______________________________   **WEIGHT** _______________________________

DATE	TIME	AM	PM	SYSTOLIC – UPPER NO –	SYSTOLIC – LOWER NO –	HEART RATE	NOTE
MONDAY		AM	PM				
TUESDAY		AM	PM				
WEDNESDAY		AM	PM				
THURSDAY		AM	PM				
FRIDAY		AM	PM				
SATURDAY		AM	PM				
SUNDAY		AM	PM				

WEEK _______________________________   **WEIGHT** _______________________________

DATE	TIME	AM	PM	SYSTOLIC – UPPER NO –	SYSTOLIC – LOWER NO –	HEART RATE	NOTE
MONDAY		AM	PM				
TUESDAY		AM	PM				
WEDNESDAY		AM	PM				
THURSDAY		AM	PM				
FRIDAY		AM	PRM				
SATURDAY		AM	PM				
SUNDAY		AM	PM				

BLOOD PRESSURE LOGBOOK

WEEK .... **WEIGHT** ....

DATE	TIME	AM	PM	SYSTOLIC – UPPER NO –	SYSTOLIC – LOWER NO –	HEART RATE	NOTE
MONDAY		AM	PM				
TUESDAY		AM	PM				
WEDNESDAY		AM	PM				
THURSDAY		AM	PM				
FRIDAY		AM	PM				
SATURDAY		AM	PM				
SUNDAY		AM	PM				

WEEK .... **WEIGHT** ....

DATE	TIME	AM	PM	SYSTOLIC – UPPER NO –	SYSTOLIC – LOWER NO –	HEART RATE	NOTE
MONDAY		AM	PM				
TUESDAY		AM	PM				
WEDNESDAY		AM	PM				
THURSDAY		AM	PM				
FRIDAY		AM	PM				
SATURDAY		AM	PM				
SUNDAY		AM	PM				

BLOOD
PRESSURE LOGBOOK

WEEK ________________________ **WEIGHT** ________________________

DATE	TIME	AM	PM	SYSTOLIC – UPPER NO –	SYSTOLIC – LOWER NO –	HEART RATE	NOTE
MONDAY		AM	PM				
TUESDAY		AM	PM				
WEDNESDAY		AM	PM				
THURSDAY		AM	PM				
FRIDAY		AM	PM				
SATURDAY		AM	PM				
SUNDAY		AM	PM				

WEEK ________________________ **WEIGHT** ________________________

DATE	TIME	AM	PM	SYSTOLIC – UPPER NO –	SYSTOLIC – LOWER NO –	HEART RATE	NOTE
MONDAY		AM	PM				
TUESDAY		AM	PM				
WEDNESDAY		AM	PM				
THURSDAY		AM	PM				
FRIDAY		AM	PRM				
SATURDAY		AM	PM				
SUNDAY		AM	PM				

BLOOD
PRESSURE LOGBOOK

WEEK .... WEIGHT ....

DATE	TIME	AM	PM	SYSTOLIC – UPPER NO –	SYSTOLIC – LOWER NO –	HEART RATE	NOTE
MONDAY		AM	PM				
TUESDAY		AM	PM				
WEDNESDAY		AM	PM				
THURSDAY		AM	PM				
FRIDAY		AM	PM				
SATURDAY		AM	PM				
SUNDAY		AM	PM				

WEEK .... WEIGHT ....

DATE	TIME	AM	PM	SYSTOLIC – UPPER NO –	SYSTOLIC – LOWER NO –	HEART RATE	NOTE
MONDAY		AM	PM				
TUESDAY		AM	PM				
WEDNESDAY		AM	PM				
THURSDAY		AM	PM				
FRIDAY		AM	PM				
SATURDAY		AM	PM				
SUNDAY		AM	PM				

BLOOD
PRESSURE LOGBOOK

WEEK ________________________ **WEIGHT** ________________________

DATE	TIME	AM	PM	SYSTOLIC – UPPER NO –	SYSTOLIC – LOWER NO –	HEART RATE	NOTE
MONDAY		AM	PM				
TUESDAY		AM	PM				
WEDNESDAY		AM	PM				
THURSDAY		AM	PM				
FRIDAY		AM	PM				
SATURDAY		AM	PM				
SUNDAY		AM	PM				

WEEK ________________________ **WEIGHT** ________________________

DATE	TIME	AM	PM	SYSTOLIC – UPPER NO –	SYSTOLIC – LOWER NO –	HEART RATE	NOTE
MONDAY		AM	PM				
TUESDAY		AM	PM				
WEDNESDAY		AM	PM				
THURSDAY		AM	PM				
FRIDAY		AM	PRM				
SATURDAY		AM	PM				
SUNDAY		AM	PM				

BLOOD
PRESSURE LOGBOOK

WEEK .... **WEIGHT** ....

DATE	TIME	AM	PM	SYSTOLIC – UPPER NO –	SYSTOLIC – LOWER NO –	HEART RATE	NOTE
MONDAY		AM	PM				
TUESDAY		AM	PM				
WEDNESDAY		AM	PM				
THURSDAY		AM	PM				
FRIDAY		AM	PM				
SATURDAY		AM	PM				
SUNDAY		AM	PM				

WEEK .... **WEIGHT** ....

DATE	TIME	AM	PM	SYSTOLIC – UPPER NO –	SYSTOLIC – LOWER NO –	HEART RATE	NOTE
MONDAY		AM	PM				
TUESDAY		AM	PM				
WEDNESDAY		AM	PM				
THURSDAY		AM	PM				
FRIDAY		AM	PM				
SATURDAY		AM	PM				
SUNDAY		AM	PM				

BLOOD
PRESSURE LOGBOOK

WEEK _______________________ WEIGHT _______________________

DATE	TIME	AM	PM	SYSTOLIC ~ UPPER NO ~	SYSTOLIC ~ LOWER NO ~	HEART RATE	NOTE
MONDAY		AM	PM				
TUESDAY		AM	PM				
WEDNESDAY		AM	PM				
THURSDAY		AM	PM				
FRIDAY		AM	PM				
SATURDAY		AM	PM				
SUNDAY		AM	PM				

WEEK _______________________ WEIGHT _______________________

DATE	TIME	AM	PM	SYSTOLIC ~ UPPER NO ~	SYSTOLIC ~ LOWER NO ~	HEART RATE	NOTE
MONDAY		AM	PM				
TUESDAY		AM	PM				
WEDNESDAY		AM	PM				
THURSDAY		AM	PM				
FRIDAY		AM	PRM				
SATURDAY		AM	PM				
SUNDAY		AM	PM				

BLOOD PRESSURE LOGBOOK

WEEK .... **WEIGHT** ....

DATE	TIME	AM	PM	SYSTOLIC – UPPER NO –	SYSTOLIC – LOWER NO –	HEART RATE	NOTE
MONDAY		AM	PM				
TUESDAY		AM	PM				
WEDNESDAY		AM	PM				
THURSDAY		AM	PM				
FRIDAY		AM	PM				
SATURDAY		AM	PM				
SUNDAY		AM	PM				

WEEK .... **WEIGHT** ....

DATE	TIME	AM	PM	SYSTOLIC – UPPER NO –	SYSTOLIC – LOWER NO –	HEART RATE	NOTE
MONDAY		AM	PM				
TUESDAY		AM	PM				
WEDNESDAY		AM	PM				
THURSDAY		AM	PM				
FRIDAY		AM	PM				
SATURDAY		AM	PM				
SUNDAY		AM	PM				

BLOOD
PRESSURE LOGBOOK

WEEK .... **WEIGHT** ....

DATE	TIME	AM	PM	SYSTOLIC – UPPER NO –	SYSTOLIC – LOWER NO –	HEART RATE	NOTE
MONDAY		AM	PM				
TUESDAY		AM	PM				
WEDNESDAY		AM	PM				
THURSDAY		AM	PM				
FRIDAY		AM	PM				
SATURDAY		AM	PM				
SUNDAY		AM	PM				

WEEK .... **WEIGHT** ....

DATE	TIME	AM	PM	SYSTOLIC – UPPER NO –	SYSTOLIC – LOWER NO –	HEART RATE	NOTE
MONDAY		AM	PM				
TUESDAY		AM	PM				
WEDNESDAY		AM	PM				
THURSDAY		AM	PM				
FRIDAY		AM	PM				
SATURDAY		AM	PM				
SUNDAY		AM	PM				

BLOOD
PRESSURE LOGBOOK

WEEK _________________________ WEIGHT _________________________

DATE	TIME	AM	PM	SYSTOLIC – UPPER NO –	SYSTOLIC – LOWER NO –	HEART RATE	NOTE
MONDAY		AM	PM				
TUESDAY		AM	PM				
WEDNESDAY		AM	PM				
THURSDAY		AM	PM				
FRIDAY		AM	PM				
SATURDAY		AM	PM				
SUNDAY		AM	PM				

WEEK _________________________ WEIGHT _________________________

DATE	TIME	AM	PM	SYSTOLIC – UPPER NO –	SYSTOLIC – LOWER NO –	HEART RATE	NOTE
MONDAY		AM	PM				
TUESDAY		AM	PM				
WEDNESDAY		AM	PM				
THURSDAY		AM	PM				
FRIDAY		AM	PM				
SATURDAY		AM	PM				
SUNDAY		AM	PM				

BLOOD
PRESSURE LOGBOOK

WEEK _______________________ **WEIGHT** _______________________

DATE	TIME	AM	PM	SYSTOLIC – UPPER NO –	SYSTOLIC – LOWER NO –	HEART RATE	NOTE
MONDAY		AM	PM				
TUESDAY		AM	PM				
WEDNESDAY		AM	PM				
THURSDAY		AM	PM				
FRIDAY		AM	PM				
SATURDAY		AM	PM				
SUNDAY		AM	PM				

WEEK _______________________ **WEIGHT** _______________________

DATE	TIME	AM	PM	SYSTOLIC – UPPER NO –	SYSTOLIC – LOWER NO –	HEART RATE	NOTE
MONDAY		AM	PM				
TUESDAY		AM	PM				
WEDNESDAY		AM	PM				
THURSDAY		AM	PM				
FRIDAY		AM	PM				
SATURDAY		AM	PM				
SUNDAY		AM	PM				

BLOOD
PRESSURE LOGBOOK

WEEK _________________________   WEIGHT _________________________

DATE	TIME	AM	PM	SYSTOLIC – UPPER NO –	SYSTOLIC – LOWER NO –	HEART RATE	NOTE
MONDAY		AM	PM				
TUESDAY		AM	PM				
WEDNESDAY		AM	PM				
THURSDAY		AM	PM				
FRIDAY		AM	PM				
SATURDAY		AM	PM				
SUNDAY		AM	PM				

WEEK _________________________   WEIGHT _________________________

DATE	TIME	AM	PM	SYSTOLIC – UPPER NO –	SYSTOLIC – LOWER NO –	HEART RATE	NOTE
MONDAY		AM	PM				
TUESDAY		AM	PM				
WEDNESDAY		AM	PM				
THURSDAY		AM	PM				
FRIDAY		AM	PM				
SATURDAY		AM	PM				
SUNDAY		AM	PM				

BLOOD
PRESSURE LOGBOOK

WEEK .... **WEIGHT** ....

DATE	TIME	AM	PM	SYSTOLIC – UPPER NO –	SYSTOLIC – LOWER NO –	HEART RATE	NOTE
MONDAY		AM	PM				
TUESDAY		AM	PM				
WEDNESDAY		AM	PM				
THURSDAY		AM	PM				
FRIDAY		AM	PM				
SATURDAY		AM	PM				
SUNDAY		AM	PM				

WEEK .... **WEIGHT** ....

DATE	TIME	AM	PM	SYSTOLIC – UPPER NO –	SYSTOLIC – LOWER NO –	HEART RATE	NOTE
MONDAY		AM	PM				
TUESDAY		AM	PM				
WEDNESDAY		AM	PM				
THURSDAY		AM	PM				
FRIDAY		AM	PM				
SATURDAY		AM	PM				
SUNDAY		AM	PM				

BLOOD
PRESSURE LOGBOOK

WEEK .... **WEIGHT** ....

DATE	TIME	AM	PM	SYSTOLIC – UPPER NO –	SYSTOLIC – LOWER NO –	HEART RATE	NOTE
MONDAY		AM	PM				
TUESDAY		AM	PM				
WEDNESDAY		AM	PM				
THURSDAY		AM	PM				
FRIDAY		AM	PM				
SATURDAY		AM	PM				
SUNDAY		AM	PM				

WEEK .... **WEIGHT** ....

DATE	TIME	AM	PM	SYSTOLIC – UPPER NO –	SYSTOLIC – LOWER NO –	HEART RATE	NOTE
MONDAY		AM	PM				
TUESDAY		AM	PM				
WEDNESDAY		AM	PM				
THURSDAY		AM	PM				
FRIDAY		AM	PRM				
SATURDAY		AM	PM				
SUNDAY		AM	PM				

BLOOD
PRESSURE LOGBOOK

WEEK _____________________ **WEIGHT** _____________________

DATE	TIME	AM	PM	SYSTOLIC – UPPER NO –	SYSTOLIC – LOWER NO –	HEART RATE	NOTE
MONDAY		AM	PM				
TUESDAY		AM	PM				
WEDNESDAY		AM	PM				
THURSDAY		AM	PM				
FRIDAY		AM	PM				
SATURDAY		AM	PM				
SUNDAY		AM	PM				

WEEK _____________________ **WEIGHT** _____________________

DATE	TIME	AM	PM	SYSTOLIC – UPPER NO –	SYSTOLIC – LOWER NO –	HEART RATE	NOTE
MONDAY		AM	PM				
TUESDAY		AM	PM				
WEDNESDAY		AM	PM				
THURSDAY		AM	PM				
FRIDAY		AM	PM				
SATURDAY		AM	PM				
SUNDAY		AM	PM				

BLOOD
PRESSURE LOGBOOK

WEEK .... **WEIGHT** ....

DATE	TIME	AM	PM	SYSTOLIC – UPPER NO –	SYSTOLIC – LOWER NO –	HEART RATE	NOTE
MONDAY		AM	PM				
TUESDAY		AM	PM				
WEDNESDAY		AM	PM				
THURSDAY		AM	PM				
FRIDAY		AM	PM				
SATURDAY		AM	PM				
SUNDAY		AM	PM				

WEEK .... **WEIGHT** ....

DATE	TIME	AM	PM	SYSTOLIC – UPPER NO –	SYSTOLIC – LOWER NO –	HEART RATE	NOTE
MONDAY		AM	PM				
TUESDAY		AM	PM				
WEDNESDAY		AM	PM				
THURSDAY		AM	PM				
FRIDAY		AM	PM				
SATURDAY		AM	PM				
SUNDAY		AM	PM				

BLOOD
PRESSURE LOGBOOK

WEEK .... **WEIGHT** ....

DATE	TIME	AM	PM	SYSTOLIC – UPPER NO –	SYSTOLIC – LOWER NO –	HEART RATE	NOTE
MONDAY		AM	PM				
TUESDAY		AM	PM				
WEDNESDAY		AM	PM				
THURSDAY		AM	PM				
FRIDAY		AM	PM				
SATURDAY		AM	PM				
SUNDAY		AM	PM				

WEEK .... **WEIGHT** ....

DATE	TIME	AM	PM	SYSTOLIC – UPPER NO –	SYSTOLIC – LOWER NO –	HEART RATE	NOTE
MONDAY		AM	PM				
TUESDAY		AM	PM				
WEDNESDAY		AM	PM				
THURSDAY		AM	PM				
FRIDAY		AM	PM				
SATURDAY		AM	PM				
SUNDAY		AM	PM				

BLOOD
PRESSURE LOGBOOK

WEEK _________________________ WEIGHT _________________________

DATE	TIME	AM	PM	SYSTOLIC – UPPER NO –	SYSTOLIC – LOWER NO –	HEART RATE	NOTE
MONDAY		AM	PM				
TUESDAY		AM	PM				
WEDNESDAY		AM	PM				
THURSDAY		AM	PM				
FRIDAY		AM	PM				
SATURDAY		AM	PM				
SUNDAY		AM	PM				

WEEK _________________________ WEIGHT _________________________

DATE	TIME	AM	PM	SYSTOLIC – UPPER NO –	SYSTOLIC – LOWER NO –	HEART RATE	NOTE
MONDAY		AM	PM				
TUESDAY		AM	PM				
WEDNESDAY		AM	PM				
THURSDAY		AM	PM				
FRIDAY		AM	PM				
SATURDAY		AM	PM				
SUNDAY		AM	PM				

BLOOD
PRESSURE LOGBOOK

WEEK ______________________________ **WEIGHT** ______________________________

DATE	TIME	AM	PM	SYSTOLIC – UPPER NO –	SYSTOLIC – LOWER NO –	HEART RATE	NOTE
MONDAY		AM	PM				
TUESDAY		AM	PM				
WEDNESDAY		AM	PM				
THURSDAY		AM	PM				
FRIDAY		AM	PM				
SATURDAY		AM	PM				
SUNDAY		AM	PM				

WEEK ______________________________ **WEIGHT** ______________________________

DATE	TIME	AM	PM	SYSTOLIC – UPPER NO –	SYSTOLIC – LOWER NO –	HEART RATE	NOTE
MONDAY		AM	PM				
TUESDAY		AM	PM				
WEDNESDAY		AM	PM				
THURSDAY		AM	PM				
FRIDAY		AM	PM				
SATURDAY		AM	PM				
SUNDAY		AM	PM				

BLOOD
PRESSURE LOGBOOK

WEEK ______________________________ **WEIGHT** ______________________________

DATE	TIME	AM	PM	SYSTOLIC – UPPER NO –	SYSTOLIC – LOWER NO –	HEART RATE	NOTE
MONDAY		AM	PM				
TUESDAY		AM	PM				
WEDNESDAY		AM	PM				
THURSDAY		AM	PM				
FRIDAY		AM	PM				
SATURDAY		AM	PM				
SUNDAY		AM	PM				

WEEK ______________________________ **WEIGHT** ______________________________

DATE	TIME	AM	PM	SYSTOLIC – UPPER NO –	SYSTOLIC – LOWER NO –	HEART RATE	NOTE
MONDAY		AM	PM				
TUESDAY		AM	PM				
WEDNESDAY		AM	PM				
THURSDAY		AM	PM				
FRIDAY		AM	PM				
SATURDAY		AM	PM				
SUNDAY		AM	PM				

BLOOD PRESSURE LOGBOOK

WEEK _______________________________ **WEIGHT** _______________________________

DATE	TIME	AM	PM	SYSTOLIC – UPPER NO –	SYSTOLIC – LOWER NO –	HEART RATE	NOTE
MONDAY		AM	PM				
TUESDAY		AM	PM				
WEDNESDAY		AM	PM				
THURSDAY		AM	PM				
FRIDAY		AM	PM				
SATURDAY		AM	PM				
SUNDAY		AM	PM				

WEEK _______________________________ **WEIGHT** _______________________________

DATE	TIME	AM	PM	SYSTOLIC – UPPER NO –	SYSTOLIC – LOWER NO –	HEART RATE	NOTE
MONDAY		AM	PM				
TUESDAY		AM	PM				
WEDNESDAY		AM	PM				
THURSDAY		AM	PM				
FRIDAY		AM	PM				
SATURDAY		AM	PM				
SUNDAY		AM	PM				

BLOOD PRESSURE LOGBOOK

WEEK .... **WEIGHT** ....

DATE	TIME	AM	PM	SYSTOLIC – UPPER NO –	SYSTOLIC – LOWER NO –	HEART RATE	NOTE
MONDAY		AM	PM				
TUESDAY		AM	PM				
WEDNESDAY		AM	PM				
THURSDAY		AM	PM				
FRIDAY		AM	PM				
SATURDAY		AM	PM				
SUNDAY		AM	PM				

WEEK .... **WEIGHT** ....

DATE	TIME	AM	PM	SYSTOLIC – UPPER NO –	SYSTOLIC – LOWER NO –	HEART RATE	NOTE
MONDAY		AM	PM				
TUESDAY		AM	PM				
WEDNESDAY		AM	PM				
THURSDAY		AM	PM				
FRIDAY		AM	PM				
SATURDAY		AM	PM				
SUNDAY		AM	PM				

BLOOD
PRESSURE LOGBOOK

WEEK ________________________________   WEIGHT ________________________________

DATE	TIME	AM	PM	SYSTOLIC – UPPER NO –	SYSTOLIC – LOWER NO –	HEART RATE	NOTE
MONDAY		AM	PM				
TUESDAY		AM	PM				
WEDNESDAY		AM	PM				
THURSDAY		AM	PM				
FRIDAY		AM	PM				
SATURDAY		AM	PM				
SUNDAY		AM	PM				

WEEK ________________________________   WEIGHT ________________________________

DATE	TIME	AM	PM	SYSTOLIC – UPPER NO –	SYSTOLIC – LOWER NO –	HEART RATE	NOTE
MONDAY		AM	PM				
TUESDAY		AM	PM				
WEDNESDAY		AM	PM				
THURSDAY		AM	PM				
FRIDAY		AM	PRESS				
SATURDAY		AM	PM				
SUNDAY		AM	PM				

BLOOD
PRESSURE LOGBOOK

WEEK .... WEIGHT ....

DATE	TIME	AM	PM	SYSTOLIC – UPPER NO –	SYSTOLIC – LOWER NO –	HEART RATE	NOTE
MONDAY		AM	PM				
TUESDAY		AM	PM				
WEDNESDAY		AM	PM				
THURSDAY		AM	PM				
FRIDAY		AM	PM				
SATURDAY		AM	PM				
SUNDAY		AM	PM				

WEEK .... WEIGHT ....

DATE	TIME	AM	PM	SYSTOLIC – UPPER NO –	SYSTOLIC – LOWER NO –	HEART RATE	NOTE
MONDAY		AM	PM				
TUESDAY		AM	PM				
WEDNESDAY		AM	PM				
THURSDAY		AM	PM				
FRIDAY		AM	PM				
SATURDAY		AM	PM				
SUNDAY		AM	PM				

BLOOD
PRESSURE LOGBOOK

WEEK ______________________ WEIGHT ______________________

DATE	TIME	AM	PM	SYSTOLIC – UPPER NO –	SYSTOLIC – LOWER NO –	HEART RATE	NOTE
MONDAY		AM	PM				
TUESDAY		AM	PM				
WEDNESDAY		AM	PM				
THURSDAY		AM	PM				
FRIDAY		AM	PM				
SATURDAY		AM	PM				
SUNDAY		AM	PM				

WEEK ______________________ WEIGHT ______________________

DATE	TIME	AM	PM	SYSTOLIC – UPPER NO –	SYSTOLIC – LOWER NO –	HEART RATE	NOTE
MONDAY		AM	PM				
TUESDAY		AM	PM				
WEDNESDAY		AM	PM				
THURSDAY		AM	PM				
FRIDAY		AM	PM				
SATURDAY		AM	PM				
SUNDAY		AM	PM				

BLOOD PRESSURE LOGBOOK

WEEK .... WEIGHT ....

DATE	TIME	AM	PM	SYSTOLIC – UPPER NO –	SYSTOLIC – LOWER NO –	HEART RATE	NOTE
MONDAY		AM	PM				
TUESDAY		AM	PM				
WEDNESDAY		AM	PM				
THURSDAY		AM	PM				
FRIDAY		AM	PM				
SATURDAY		AM	PM				
SUNDAY		AM	PM				

WEEK .... WEIGHT ....

DATE	TIME	AM	PM	SYSTOLIC – UPPER NO –	SYSTOLIC – LOWER NO –	HEART RATE	NOTE
MONDAY		AM	PM				
TUESDAY		AM	PM				
WEDNESDAY		AM	PM				
THURSDAY		AM	PM				
FRIDAY		AM	PM				
SATURDAY		AM	PM				
SUNDAY		AM	PM				

BLOOD PRESSURE LOGBOOK

WEEK _____________________ WEIGHT _____________________

DATE	TIME	AM	PM	SYSTOLIC – UPPER NO –	SYSTOLIC – LOWER NO –	HEART RATE	NOTE
MONDAY		AM	PM				
TUESDAY		AM	PM				
WEDNESDAY		AM	PM				
THURSDAY		AM	PM				
FRIDAY		AM	PM				
SATURDAY		AM	PM				
SUNDAY		AM	PM				

WEEK _____________________ WEIGHT _____________________

DATE	TIME	AM	PM	SYSTOLIC – UPPER NO –	SYSTOLIC – LOWER NO –	HEART RATE	NOTE
MONDAY		AM	PM				
TUESDAY		AM	PM				
WEDNESDAY		AM	PM				
THURSDAY		AM	PM				
FRIDAY		AM	PM				
SATURDAY		AM	PM				
SUNDAY		AM	PM				

BLOOD
PRESSURE LOGBOOK

WEEK .... WEIGHT ....

DATE	TIME	AM	PM	SYSTOLIC – UPPER NO –	SYSTOLIC – LOWER NO –	HEART RATE	NOTE
MONDAY		AM	PM				
TUESDAY		AM	PM				
WEDNESDAY		AM	PM				
THURSDAY		AM	PM				
FRIDAY		AM	PM				
SATURDAY		AM	PM				
SUNDAY		AM	PM				

WEEK .... WEIGHT ....

DATE	TIME	AM	PM	SYSTOLIC – UPPER NO –	SYSTOLIC – LOWER NO –	HEART RATE	NOTE
MONDAY		AM	PM				
TUESDAY		AM	PM				
WEDNESDAY		AM	PM				
THURSDAY		AM	PM				
FRIDAY		AM	PM				
SATURDAY		AM	PM				
SUNDAY		AM	PM				

BLOOD PRESSURE LOGBOOK

WEEK ________________________   WEIGHT ________________________

DATE	TIME	AM	PM	SYSTOLIC – UPPER NO –	SYSTOLIC – LOWER NO –	HEART RATE	NOTE
MONDAY		AM	PM				
TUESDAY		AM	PM				
WEDNESDAY		AM	PM				
THURSDAY		AM	PM				
FRIDAY		AM	PM				
SATURDAY		AM	PM				
SUNDAY		AM	PM				

WEEK ________________________   WEIGHT ________________________

DATE	TIME	AM	PM	SYSTOLIC – UPPER NO –	SYSTOLIC – LOWER NO –	HEART RATE	NOTE
MONDAY		AM	PM				
TUESDAY		AM	PM				
WEDNESDAY		AM	PM				
THURSDAY		AM	PM				
FRIDAY		AM	PM				
SATURDAY		AM	PM				
SUNDAY		AM	PM				

BLOOD
PRESSURE LOGBOOK

WEEK .... WEIGHT ....

DATE	TIME	AM	PM	SYSTOLIC ~ UPPER NO ~	SYSTOLIC ~ LOWER NO ~	HEART RATE	NOTE
MONDAY		AM	PM				
TUESDAY		AM	PM				
WEDNESDAY		AM	PM				
THURSDAY		AM	PM				
FRIDAY		AM	PM				
SATURDAY		AM	PM				
SUNDAY		AM	PM				

WEEK .... WEIGHT ....

DATE	TIME	AM	PM	SYSTOLIC ~ UPPER NO ~	SYSTOLIC ~ LOWER NO ~	HEART RATE	NOTE
MONDAY		AM	PM				
TUESDAY		AM	PM				
WEDNESDAY		AM	PM				
THURSDAY		AM	PM				
FRIDAY		AM	PRM				
SATURDAY		AM	PM				
SUNDAY		AM	PM				

BLOOD
PRESSURE LOGBOOK

WEEK _______________________________   **WEIGHT** _______________________________

DATE	TIME	AM	PM	SYSTOLIC - UPPER NO -	SYSTOLIC - LOWER NO -	HEART RATE	NOTE
MONDAY		AM	PM				
TUESDAY		AM	PM				
WEDNESDAY		AM	PM				
THURSDAY		AM	PM				
FRIDAY		AM	PM				
SATURDAY		AM	PM				
SUNDAY		AM	PM				

WEEK _______________________________   **WEIGHT** _______________________________

DATE	TIME	AM	PM	SYSTOLIC - UPPER NO -	SYSTOLIC - LOWER NO -	HEART RATE	NOTE
MONDAY		AM	PM				
TUESDAY		AM	PM				
WEDNESDAY		AM	PM				
THURSDAY		AM	PM				
FRIDAY		AM	PRM				
SATURDAY		AM	PM				
SUNDAY		AM	PM				

BLOOD PRESSURE LOGBOOK

WEEK _____________________________ WEIGHT _____________________________

DATE	TIME	AM	PM	SYSTOLIC – UPPER NO –	SYSTOLIC – LOWER NO –	HEART RATE	NOTE
MONDAY		AM	PM				
TUESDAY		AM	PM				
WEDNESDAY		AM	PM				
THURSDAY		AM	PM				
FRIDAY		AM	PM				
SATURDAY		AM	PM				
SUNDAY		AM	PM				

WEEK _____________________________ WEIGHT _____________________________

DATE	TIME	AM	PM	SYSTOLIC – UPPER NO –	SYSTOLIC – LOWER NO –	HEART RATE	NOTE
MONDAY		AM	PM				
TUESDAY		AM	PM				
WEDNESDAY		AM	PM				
THURSDAY		AM	PM				
FRIDAY		AM	PM				
SATURDAY		AM	PM				
SUNDAY		AM	PM				

BLOOD
PRESSURE LOGBOOK

WEEK _____________________________ WEIGHT _____________________________

DATE	TIME	AM	PM	SYSTOLIC – UPPER NO –	SYSTOLIC – LOWER NO –	HEART RATE	NOTE
MONDAY		AM	PM				
TUESDAY		AM	PM				
WEDNESDAY		AM	PM				
THURSDAY		AM	PM				
FRIDAY		AM	PM				
SATURDAY		AM	PM				
SUNDAY		AM	PM				

WEEK _____________________________ WEIGHT _____________________________

DATE	TIME	AM	PM	SYSTOLIC – UPPER NO –	SYSTOLIC – LOWER NO –	HEART RATE	NOTE
MONDAY		AM	PM				
TUESDAY		AM	PM				
WEDNESDAY		AM	PM				
THURSDAY		AM	PM				
FRIDAY		AM	PM				
SATURDAY		AM	PM				
SUNDAY		AM	PM				

BLOOD
PRESSURE LOGBOOK

WEEK .... **WEIGHT** ....

DATE	TIME	AM	PM	SYSTOLIC – UPPER NO –	SYSTOLIC – LOWER NO –	HEART RATE	NOTE
MONDAY		AM	PM				
TUESDAY		AM	PM				
WEDNESDAY		AM	PM				
THURSDAY		AM	PM				
FRIDAY		AM	PM				
SATURDAY		AM	PM				
SUNDAY		AM	PM				

WEEK .... **WEIGHT** ....

DATE	TIME	AM	PM	SYSTOLIC – UPPER NO –	SYSTOLIC – LOWER NO –	HEART RATE	NOTE
MONDAY		AM	PM				
TUESDAY		AM	PM				
WEDNESDAY		AM	PM				
THURSDAY		AM	PM				
FRIDAY		AM	PM				
SATURDAY		AM	PM				
SUNDAY		AM	PM				

BLOOD PRESSURE LOGBOOK

WEEK _______________________________ **WEIGHT** _______________________________

DATE	TIME	AM	PM	SYSTOLIC – UPPER NO –	SYSTOLIC – LOWER NO –	HEART RATE	NOTE
MONDAY		AM	PM				
TUESDAY		AM	PM				
WEDNESDAY		AM	PM				
THURSDAY		AM	PM				
FRIDAY		AM	PM				
SATURDAY		AM	PM				
SUNDAY		AM	PM				

WEEK _______________________________ **WEIGHT** _______________________________

DATE	TIME	AM	PM	SYSTOLIC – UPPER NO –	SYSTOLIC – LOWER NO –	HEART RATE	NOTE
MONDAY		AM	PM				
TUESDAY		AM	PM				
WEDNESDAY		AM	PM				
THURSDAY		AM	PM				
FRIDAY		AM	PM				
SATURDAY		AM	PM				
SUNDAY		AM	PM				

BLOOD PRESSURE LOGBOOK

WEEK .... **WEIGHT** ....

DATE	TIME	AM	PM	SYSTOLIC – UPPER NO –	SYSTOLIC – LOWER NO –	HEART RATE	NOTE
MONDAY		AM	PM				
TUESDAY		AM	PM				
WEDNESDAY		AM	PM				
THURSDAY		AM	PM				
FRIDAY		AM	PM				
SATURDAY		AM	PM				
SUNDAY		AM	PM				

WEEK .... **WEIGHT** ....

DATE	TIME	AM	PM	SYSTOLIC – UPPER NO –	SYSTOLIC – LOWER NO –	HEART RATE	NOTE
MONDAY		AM	PM				
TUESDAY		AM	PM				
WEDNESDAY		AM	PM				
THURSDAY		AM	PM				
FRIDAY		AM	PM				
SATURDAY		AM	PM				
SUNDAY		AM	PM				

BLOOD
PRESSURE LOGBOOK

WEEK ______________________________ **WEIGHT** ______________________________

DATE	TIME	AM	PM	SYSTOLIC – UPPER NO –	SYSTOLIC – LOWER NO –	HEART RATE	NOTE
MONDAY		AM	PM				
TUESDAY		AM	PM				
WEDNESDAY		AM	PM				
THURSDAY		AM	PM				
FRIDAY		AM	PM				
SATURDAY		AM	PM				
SUNDAY		AM	PM				

WEEK ______________________________ **WEIGHT** ______________________________

DATE	TIME	AM	PM	SYSTOLIC – UPPER NO –	SYSTOLIC – LOWER NO –	HEART RATE	NOTE
MONDAY		AM	PM				
TUESDAY		AM	PM				
WEDNESDAY		AM	PM				
THURSDAY		AM	PM				
FRIDAY		AM	PM				
SATURDAY		AM	PM				
SUNDAY		AM	PM				

BLOOD
PRESSURE LOGBOOK

WEEK ___________________________ **WEIGHT** ___________________________

DATE	TIME	AM	PM	SYSTOLIC – UPPER NO –	SYSTOLIC – LOWER NO –	HEART RATE	NOTE
MONDAY		AM	PM				
TUESDAY		AM	PM				
WEDNESDAY		AM	PM				
THURSDAY		AM	PM				
FRIDAY		AM	PM				
SATURDAY		AM	PM				
SUNDAY		AM	PM				

WEEK ___________________________ **WEIGHT** ___________________________

DATE	TIME	AM	PM	SYSTOLIC – UPPER NO –	SYSTOLIC – LOWER NO –	HEART RATE	NOTE
MONDAY		AM	PM				
TUESDAY		AM	PM				
WEDNESDAY		AM	PM				
THURSDAY		AM	PM				
FRIDAY		AM	PM				
SATURDAY		AM	PM				
SUNDAY		AM	PM				

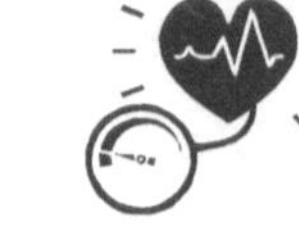

BLOOD
PRESSURE LOGBOOK

WEEK ________________________ **WEIGHT** ________________________

DATE	TIME	AM	PM	SYSTOLIC – UPPER NO –	SYSTOLIC – LOWER NO –	HEART RATE	NOTE
MONDAY		AM	PM				
TUESDAY		AM	PM				
WEDNESDAY		AM	PM				
THURSDAY		AM	PM				
FRIDAY		AM	PM				
SATURDAY		AM	PM				
SUNDAY		AM	PM				

WEEK ________________________ **WEIGHT** ________________________

DATE	TIME	AM	PM	SYSTOLIC – UPPER NO –	SYSTOLIC – LOWER NO –	HEART RATE	NOTE
MONDAY		AM	PM				
TUESDAY		AM	PM				
WEDNESDAY		AM	PM				
THURSDAY		AM	PM				
FRIDAY		AM	PM				
SATURDAY		AM	PM				
SUNDAY		AM	PM				

BLOOD
PRESSURE LOGBOOK

WEEK ____________________________ **WEIGHT** ____________________________

DATE	TIME	AM	PM	SYSTOLIC – UPPER NO –	SYSTOLIC – LOWER NO –	HEART RATE	NOTE
MONDAY		AM	PM				
TUESDAY		AM	PM				
WEDNESDAY		AM	PM				
THURSDAY		AM	PM				
FRIDAY		AM	PM				
SATURDAY		AM	PM				
SUNDAY		AM	PM				

WEEK ____________________________ **WEIGHT** ____________________________

DATE	TIME	AM	PM	SYSTOLIC – UPPER NO –	SYSTOLIC – LOWER NO –	HEART RATE	NOTE
MONDAY		AM	PM				
TUESDAY		AM	PM				
WEDNESDAY		AM	PM				
THURSDAY		AM	PM				
FRIDAY		AM	PM				
SATURDAY		AM	PM				
SUNDAY		AM	PM				

BLOOD
PRESSURE LOGBOOK

WEEK _____________________ **WEIGHT** _____________________

DATE	TIME	AM	PM	SYSTOLIC – UPPER NO –	SYSTOLIC – LOWER NO –	HEART RATE	NOTE
MONDAY		AM	PM				
TUESDAY		AM	PM				
WEDNESDAY		AM	PM				
THURSDAY		AM	PM				
FRIDAY		AM	PM				
SATURDAY		AM	PM				
SUNDAY		AM	PM				

WEEK _____________________ **WEIGHT** _____________________

DATE	TIME	AM	PM	SYSTOLIC – UPPER NO –	SYSTOLIC – LOWER NO –	HEART RATE	NOTE
MONDAY		AM	PM				
TUESDAY		AM	PM				
WEDNESDAY		AM	PM				
THURSDAY		AM	PM				
FRIDAY		AM	PM				
SATURDAY		AM	PM				
SUNDAY		AM	PM				

BLOOD
PRESSURE LOGBOOK

WEEK .... **WEIGHT** ....

DATE	TIME	AM	PM	SYSTOLIC – UPPER NO –	SYSTOLIC – LOWER NO –	HEART RATE	NOTE
MONDAY		AM	PM				
TUESDAY		AM	PM				
WEDNESDAY		AM	PM				
THURSDAY		AM	PM				
FRIDAY		AM	PM				
SATURDAY		AM	PM				
SUNDAY		AM	PM				

WEEK .... **WEIGHT** ....

DATE	TIME	AM	PM	SYSTOLIC – UPPER NO –	SYSTOLIC – LOWER NO –	HEART RATE	NOTE
MONDAY		AM	PM				
TUESDAY		AM	PM				
WEDNESDAY		AM	PM				
THURSDAY		AM	PM				
FRIDAY		AM	PM				
SATURDAY		AM	PM				
SUNDAY		AM	PM				

BLOOD
PRESSURE LOGBOOK

WEEK ___________________________ WEIGHT ___________________________

DATE	TIME	AM	PM	SYSTOLIC – UPPER NO –	SYSTOLIC – LOWER NO –	HEART RATE	NOTE
MONDAY		AM	PM				
TUESDAY		AM	PM				
WEDNESDAY		AM	PM				
THURSDAY		AM	PM				
FRIDAY		AM	PM				
SATURDAY		AM	PM				
SUNDAY		AM	PM				

WEEK ___________________________ WEIGHT ___________________________

DATE	TIME	AM	PM	SYSTOLIC – UPPER NO –	SYSTOLIC – LOWER NO –	HEART RATE	NOTE
MONDAY		AM	PM				
TUESDAY		AM	PM				
WEDNESDAY		AM	PM				
THURSDAY		AM	PM				
FRIDAY		AM	PM				
SATURDAY		AM	PM				
SUNDAY		AM	PM				

BLOOD PRESSURE LOGBOOK

WEEK .... **WEIGHT** ....

DATE	TIME	AM	PM	SYSTOLIC – UPPER NO –	SYSTOLIC – LOWER NO –	HEART RATE	NOTE
MONDAY		AM	PM				
TUESDAY		AM	PM				
WEDNESDAY		AM	PM				
THURSDAY		AM	PM				
FRIDAY		AM	PM				
SATURDAY		AM	PM				
SUNDAY		AM	PM				

WEEK .... **WEIGHT** ....

DATE	TIME	AM	PM	SYSTOLIC – UPPER NO –	SYSTOLIC – LOWER NO –	HEART RATE	NOTE
MONDAY		AM	PM				
TUESDAY		AM	PM				
WEDNESDAY		AM	PM				
THURSDAY		AM	PM				
FRIDAY		AM	PM				
SATURDAY		AM	PM				
SUNDAY		AM	PM				

BLOOD PRESSURE LOGBOOK

WEEK ______________________________ **WEIGHT** ______________________________

DATE	TIME	AM	PM	SYSTOLIC – UPPER NO –	SYSTOLIC – LOWER NO –	HEART RATE	NOTE
MONDAY		AM	PM				
TUESDAY		AM	PM				
WEDNESDAY		AM	PM				
THURSDAY		AM	PM				
FRIDAY		AM	PM				
SATURDAY		AM	PM				
SUNDAY		AM	PM				

WEEK ______________________________ **WEIGHT** ______________________________

DATE	TIME	AM	PM	SYSTOLIC – UPPER NO –	SYSTOLIC – LOWER NO –	HEART RATE	NOTE
MONDAY		AM	PM				
TUESDAY		AM	PM				
WEDNESDAY		AM	PM				
THURSDAY		AM	PM				
FRIDAY		AM	PREM				
SATURDAY		AM	PM				
SUNDAY		AM	PM				

BLOOD
PRESSURE LOGBOOK

WEEK .... **WEIGHT** ....

DATE	TIME	AM	PM	SYSTOLIC - UPPER NO -	SYSTOLIC - LOWER NO -	HEART RATE	NOTE
MONDAY		AM	PM				
TUESDAY		AM	PM				
WEDNESDAY		AM	PM				
THURSDAY		AM	PM				
FRIDAY		AM	PM				
SATURDAY		AM	PM				
SUNDAY		AM	PM				

WEEK .... **WEIGHT** ....

DATE	TIME	AM	PM	SYSTOLIC - UPPER NO -	SYSTOLIC - LOWER NO -	HEART RATE	NOTE
MONDAY		AM	PM				
TUESDAY		AM	PM				
WEDNESDAY		AM	PM				
THURSDAY		AM	PM				
FRIDAY		AM	PM				
SATURDAY		AM	PM				
SUNDAY		AM	PM				

BLOOD
PRESSURE LOGBOOK

WEEK ______________________________ **WEIGHT** ______________________________

DATE	TIME	AM	PM	SYSTOLIC – UPPER NO –	SYSTOLIC – LOWER NO –	HEART RATE	NOTE
MONDAY		AM	PM				
TUESDAY		AM	PM				
WEDNESDAY		AM	PM				
THURSDAY		AM	PM				
FRIDAY		AM	PM				
SATURDAY		AM	PM				
SUNDAY		AM	PM				

WEEK ______________________________ **WEIGHT** ______________________________

DATE	TIME	AM	PM	SYSTOLIC – UPPER NO –	SYSTOLIC – LOWER NO –	HEART RATE	NOTE
MONDAY		AM	PM				
TUESDAY		AM	PM				
WEDNESDAY		AM	PM				
THURSDAY		AM	PM				
FRIDAY		AM	PRM				
SATURDAY		AM	PM				
SUNDAY		AM	PM				

BLOOD
PRESSURE LOGBOOK

WEEK _______________________________   **WEIGHT** _______________________________

DATE	TIME	AM	PM	SYSTOLIC – UPPER NO –	SYSTOLIC – LOWER NO –	HEART RATE	NOTE
MONDAY		AM	PM				
TUESDAY		AM	PM				
WEDNESDAY		AM	PM				
THURSDAY		AM	PM				
FRIDAY		AM	PM				
SATURDAY		AM	PM				
SUNDAY		AM	PM				

WEEK _______________________________   **WEIGHT** _______________________________

DATE	TIME	AM	PM	SYSTOLIC – UPPER NO –	SYSTOLIC – LOWER NO –	HEART RATE	NOTE
MONDAY		AM	PM				
TUESDAY		AM	PM				
WEDNESDAY		AM	PM				
THURSDAY		AM	PM				
FRIDAY		AM	PM				
SATURDAY		AM	PM				
SUNDAY		AM	PM				

BLOOD
PRESSURE LOGBOOK

WEEK ________________________   **WEIGHT** ________________________

DATE	TIME	AM	PM	SYSTOLIC – UPPER NO –	SYSTOLIC – LOWER NO –	HEART RATE	NOTE
MONDAY		AM	PM				
TUESDAY		AM	PM				
WEDNESDAY		AM	PM				
THURSDAY		AM	PM				
FRIDAY		AM	PM				
SATURDAY		AM	PM				
SUNDAY		AM	PM				

WEEK ________________________   **WEIGHT** ________________________

DATE	TIME	AM	PM	SYSTOLIC – UPPER NO –	SYSTOLIC – LOWER NO –	HEART RATE	NOTE
MONDAY		AM	PM				
TUESDAY		AM	PM				
WEDNESDAY		AM	PM				
THURSDAY		AM	PM				
FRIDAY		AM	PM				
SATURDAY		AM	PM				
SUNDAY		AM	PM				

BLOOD
PRESSURE LOGBOOK

WEEK .... **WEIGHT** ....

DATE	TIME	AM	PM	SYSTOLIC – UPPER NO –	SYSTOLIC – LOWER NO –	HEART RATE	NOTE
MONDAY		AM	PM				
TUESDAY		AM	PM				
WEDNESDAY		AM	PM				
THURSDAY		AM	PM				
FRIDAY		AM	PM				
SATURDAY		AM	PM				
SUNDAY		AM	PM				

WEEK .... **WEIGHT** ....

DATE	TIME	AM	PM	SYSTOLIC – UPPER NO –	SYSTOLIC – LOWER NO –	HEART RATE	NOTE
MONDAY		AM	PM				
TUESDAY		AM	PM				
WEDNESDAY		AM	PM				
THURSDAY		AM	PM				
FRIDAY		AM	PM				
SATURDAY		AM	PM				
SUNDAY		AM	PM				

BLOOD
PRESSURE LOGBOOK

WEEK .... **WEIGHT** ....

DATE	TIME	AM	PM	SYSTOLIC – UPPER NO –	SYSTOLIC – LOWER NO –	HEART RATE	NOTE
MONDAY		AM	PM				
TUESDAY		AM	PM				
WEDNESDAY		AM	PM				
THURSDAY		AM	PM				
FRIDAY		AM	PM				
SATURDAY		AM	PM				
SUNDAY		AM	PM				

WEEK .... **WEIGHT** ....

DATE	TIME	AM	PM	SYSTOLIC – UPPER NO –	SYSTOLIC – LOWER NO –	HEART RATE	NOTE
MONDAY		AM	PM				
TUESDAY		AM	PM				
WEDNESDAY		AM	PM				
THURSDAY		AM	PM				
FRIDAY		AM	PRM				
SATURDAY		AM	PM				
SUNDAY		AM	PM				

www.ingramcontent.com/pod-product-compliance
Lightning Source LLC
LaVergne TN
LVHW051444170726
843492LV00002B/532